An Unlikely Arrangement

About the author:
The daughter of a WWII Navy vet who survived Pearl Harbor, Patty Wiseman was raised in Washington State. She attended The Wesleyan College in Bartlesville, Oklahoma, and moved to Northeast Texas where she has resided for over 30 years.

Writing has been a life-long passion and in 2007, she entered the NaNoWriMo competition to write a novel in 30 days and won. She has several short stories published and is currently working on two other novels while working full time at her job of 23 years at a financial investment company. She has two grown sons and fifteen grandchildren.

Patty currently lives with her wonderful husband Ron and their dog Cutter.

An Unlikely Arrangement

Patty Wiseman

Desert Coyote Productions
Scotts Valley, California

Library of Congress Control Number 2011932580.

EAN-13: 978-1-463-62084-4
ISBN-10: 1-463-62084-5

Typeset in 11pt Book Antiqua
Printed in the U.S.A.
First edition 2011

To my husband, Ron Wiseman, for his unwavering patience and support, and unconditional love.

Acknowledgments

Set adrift
A life unknown
Connections form
Love is sown

First, I thank my husband, Ron Wiseman, my hero and greatest supporter, without whom I could never have accomplished my goal.

Heartfelt thanks go to my son, Scott Cameron, a heart so big and full of love, who encouraged me every step of the way and let his pride in my endeavor be known to everyone.

To my daughter-in-law, Jami Cameron, whose creative input and constant support lit up my imagination and let me believe in myself.

To my sister, Calla Pate, who read my stories and gave me encouragement.

To my writing partner, Jeannie Barber, a constant friend and editor, who encouraged me while we worked on a separate novel together. Her laughter and inside jokes kept me on my toes.

To my boss of 23 years, Ernie Marshall, who read my stories, made comments online, and supported me every step of the way.

To my former co-worker, Amber Hocutt, who read my stories and encouraged me to write the next chapter so she could read it.

To my critique group, Jeannie Barber, Denny and Alice Youngblood, and Lynn Hobbs, who told me the truth even if I didn't like it.

To East Texas Writers Association where I met many friends who supported and encouraged me.

And last, but certainly not least, my Editor and Publisher, Don Martinez, who made the process so much easier, and whose expertise is an asset for any writer.

Contents

An Unlikely Arrangement

Chapter One

January 1929

The voices continued ... muffled, no matter how hard her ear pressed against the thick, wooden door. *Did they say Kirby? Who is Mr. Kirby?* The crisp, winter wind shook the windowpanes, but the gooseflesh rippling on her young flesh was not a result of the cold. She pushed hard, away from the oak barrier.

"You can't do this to me, Mother. I am seventeen, a grown woman. Let me out." Ruth Squire rattled the lock while her other fist pounded the heavy door. "Do you hear me?"

No answer; she didn't expect one. She was familiar with discipline, plenty of it, the consequence of a strong will and zeal for adventure, but never like this, locked inside the second-story bedroom. Ruth's hands fell to her side. Crazy from confinement, she paced, a lioness caught in a cage.

"What is she going to do to me this time? Even Father won't talk to me." The metal springs of the bed squawked in protest at her weight. Sprawled across the rumpled bedcover she stared at the only link to the outside world. The flicker of the gas street lamp outside the warbled glass window did nothing to soothe her.

Although...*No, not the window, that is how I got in trouble in the first place.*

Alone against the world, everyone gone—her best friend Ginny, Father, and worse, she had made an enemy of Mother. Instead of rage and exasperation, her mother remained calm, determined—even sinister. "This side of her is something to fear, I believe."

The growl in her stomach intensified, and thirst ravaged her throat. *What time is it? Do they intend to keep me in here until morning with no food or drink?* A key rattled in the lock, and she jumped up as the door swung open.

Priscilla and Robert Squire entered bearing a white linen-covered tray. "You will eat now, Ruth. We'll talk after you have finished."

"I'm not hungry, take it away." Ruth's stomach lurched at the look on her father's face. His sad blue eyes showed no sign of the familiar, easy smile of assurance. Although he stood taller, he wilted beside his wife, a shadow of a man. One hand smoothed his peppered hair; the other jingled the change in his pocket.

The tray hit the nightstand with a bang. "There is no room for argument. I said eat." Mrs. Squire crossed her arms against an ample bosom.

Ruth looked to her father for help, but he only sighed, and took a seat in the chair across from her.

The warm aroma of cook's scones broke down any defiance, and her fists unclenched, although she continued to glare at both parents. She eased onto the side of the bed, hesitant, eyes on the enemy, and devoured the light, flaky scones, and warm tea in short order. The back of her hand swiped across her mouth, a move she knew Mother would abhor, and swallowed the last of the tea in one gulp.

"We have done our best to lead you on the right path. This was your last chance and now it's time for desperate measures," Mrs. Squire said.

"I wanted to have a little fun, Mother. All young people like to dance." The attempt to wiggle out of trouble would prove futile, but she tried anyway.

"I'm not interested in the other children, or the fact you value fun over responsible behavior. You are not yet eighteen, and you will not spoil my plans to have you properly married one day with a family of your own."

Ruth tossed her short black hair and poked out her chin before she spoke. "Marriage? I want to have fun, go places, and see the world. I don't want to be like you."

The pop of the slap resounded through the room. Ruth reeled backwards, held her hand to one burning cheek, and blinked in horror.

Though not tall, Priscilla Squire stood strong and broad, a stout woman, in a dark blue, shapeless dress and sensible shoes. Long, streaked, gray hair pulled back into a bun and faded, lackluster brown eyes completed the severe look.

Father sunk lower in the chair and shuddered. Mother rubbed the palm of her hand and strode toward the door…Father slinking after her like a cowed puppy. "Come morning you will have the run of the house, although Sarah's duties tomorrow include sentry and keeper of the keys. Don't try to leave, Ruth. We have arrangements to make in the morning. Now sleep."

The perfunctory remarks stunned her. "Arrangements? What arrangements? Father, what is she talking about?"

The slam of the door and turn of the key sealed her fate. Unless…*Can I get a message to my friends, Danny or Ellen? They probably wonder why I didn't show tonight. Excitement made me careless. I'll try to call in the morning. Maybe one of them will come and help me escape.* Exhaustion took over. She curled up on the bed and cried until an uneasy sleep overtook her weary body.

The jangle of the key in the lock woke her at the murky, black hour before dawn. A slow, steady throb pulsated in her head. She sat up, tried to shake the sluggish daze from her brain, and waited. *Maybe I can talk to them now. Tell them I'm sorry. Surely, they will be reasonable this morning.*

No one entered. She slipped out of bed and tried the knob. The door opened at a touch. She quickly threw on a robe and ventured into the hallway. The stairs creaked and threatened to announce her cautious escape. A quick search of the house soon confirmed her parents' absence, but she found the little Irish maid alone in the laundry room. Sarah O'Brien administered her duties flawlessly and had ever since Ruth could remember. A fixture in the family, Ruth did not consider her a servant, but a long-standing friend and confidant.

"Good morning, Sarah. So, they're gone? This time it must be serious." She waited: Sarah didn't respond. "There's nothing to do but wait in my room, I guess. That's where I'll be if you need me."

The diminutive maid continued folding the linen napkins. "Breakfast's gettin' cold in the kitchen. It'll ruin afore long."

"I'm not hungry yet, and I cannot spend the day in my robe and slippers." She hurried up the stairs, slipped into the bedroom, and closed the door. It took only a moment to pull the cotton day dress over her head and kick off the satin slippers. She opened the door a crack to make sure Sarah had not followed, took a deep breath, and tiptoed down the hall to Mother's private sanctuary—a room forbidden to her.

Once inside, her eyes adjusted to the dim light. "It smells of violets in here—such a feminine scent for my stodgy old mother. What a surprise. I wonder what else I will find. Ah, the window. Should I climb down the trellis?" In three strides, she reached the window. A quick tug of the sash and all hope dissolved. It would not budge. "Now what?" She glanced around. "I don't see the telephone anywhere, either."

Across the room, the clear glass knob on the closet door twinkled in invitation. "Naturally, the closet, a perfect hiding place." She stepped into the dark, cavern-like wardrobe. Before she found the light, the creak of a door opening frightened her. Footsteps echoed on the wooden floor.

"Ruthie Squire what in the name of everything holy are you doin'? Have you got a death wish, child? Your mum does not even let your papa in here. Come out this instant."

"All right, Sarah, I'm coming. Where did they go, by the way? They tell you everything."

"You know I cannot tell you. They would fire me for sure. Breakfast is awaitin'. Come down to the kitchen."

The temptation to trick Sarah, slam the door shut, and lock it crossed her mind. She studied the back of Sarah's head, haloed by short, blonde hair, and followed her down the stairs. It would not be fair to this woman, a friend for seventeen years. Mother would fire her. "You are right. She is a ruthless woman."

"Oh child, she's protectin' ya, is all."

"You can say what you want. You are not the one choked to death by her rules."

Sarah looked up from the bottom landing. "I live by them, too, girlie. Different ones, to be sure, but rules all the same, and they protect my job here. One day you will learn it for yourself."

"Are you going to lecture me all day or get my breakfast, Sarah O'Brien?"

"Thought you weren't hungry, girl. At any rate, your breakfast is already made, and I'll be thankin' ya to watch your tongue, or we will be addin' another crime to your long list."

"All right, all right, I'm coming."

After a quick breakfast, she thought again of the telephone, but the candlestick device continued to elude her. Mother kept constant guard on it. Father's office stayed locked. She was sure it was in the forbidden closet. Discouraged, one hand followed the smooth wood of the stair's banister back to her room. *How do I get inside Mother's room without Sarah knowing?* The afternoon passed slowly as she contemplated different scenarios of punishment until, exhausted, she plopped onto the vanity chair, grabbed her brush, and brooded over what loomed ahead of her. "Probably boarding school."

Her fingers dipped into a small pot of rouge, the one indulgence Mother allowed. "Maybe I will make myself up like a clown. They would kick me out of the stupid old boarding school right off." Her laughter filled the room. "If Mother wasn't such an old tyrant I would wear lip paint." She applied the correct amount on both cheeks, enough to give a rosy glow. "I look too young in this brown frock. Let me see…if I pull my hair back like so—yes, much better. I could pass for twenty instead of a mere seventeen."

"It is good to see you making use of your time, Ruthie."

The flimsy chair toppled as she jumped to her feet. "Mother, I didn't hear you come home."

"Prepare yourself for company. I will send Sarah up to help." Her mother's eyes narrowed—a clear warning.

"Please tell me…" Frozen, she watched her mother's ramrod straight back stiffen, but continue out of the room.

The maid appeared in the empty doorway. "Who is it, Sarah? Who is coming?"

Sarah entered the room, picked up the tortoise-shell hairbrush, and began grooming Ruth's hair. The housekeeper worked in silence, the brush rough against Ruth's scalp. The sound of horse's hooves on cobblestone and a high-pitched whinny interrupted the two women. Ruth escaped Sarah's grasp and peered through the upstairs window.

"Why is a horse-drawn milk truck parked in the alley? Sarah?" She looked over her shoulder, but the room was empty. *Sarah has turned traitor, too.* Drawn to the scene below, she peered at the sight below. "Why would a headmaster drive a milk wagon?"

The front door's brass knocker reverberated through the house. *My fate has arrived.* The voices enticed her into the hallway to listen.

"Please wait in the drawing room, Mr. Kirby. Our daughter will be down soon." Mother's voice sounded strangely light and friendly.

"Mr. Kirby?" She scurried back to the bedroom determined not to come out. A knock on the door startled her and she sat hard onto the bed, heart pounding.

Her mother swept into the room—all business. "Sarah has prepared the green dress. It is more suitable for receiving visitors. Change and be downstairs in fifteen minutes, not a moment longer."

"Who is Mr. Kirby?"

"If you want to find out you best hurry." Mrs. Squire left the room without further comment.

Alone, Ruth stared at the empty doorway. In the next instant, Sarah appeared—the freshly brushed green satin in her hand. Neither woman spoke as the homespun cotton fell to the floor. Ruth stood woodenly as Sarah pulled the green dress over her head and fastened the intricate buttons.

After a final adjustment, Sarah gave a gentle push at the small of Ruth's back. "Come on, dearie. It's not as bad as all that. Go on now, I'm right behind ya."

Tears threatened to spill over the rims of her eyes as she moved forward on leaden legs.

The conversation in the parlor sounded polite, friendly. The familiar creak of the stairs announced her approach, and her parents turned in tandem to welcome her. The parlor was a favorite room. Ornate cherrywood framed the forest green velvet sofa, a cozy place to curl up and read. Colorful flowered globes sat atop the twin oil lamps and each graced the matching end tables. Heavy, dark green drapes kept the warm afternoon sun at bay. In the corner on the settee, next to the glassed bookshelves, sat a man she thought looked too young to be a headmaster of anything, much less a school full of young women.

He stood and removed his hat, exposing sandy blond hair, bright blue eyes, a strong chin, and easy grin.

"Ruth, please greet Mr. Peter Kirby. Mr. Kirby, this is our daughter, Ruth." Mother smiled. "Mr. Kirby has agreed to marry you. The ceremony will be next week in the family church."

Chapter Two

Her hands remained clasped in front of her, settled against the soft folds of the velveteen gown; eyes downcast. Rage coursed through her body, her heart pulsed with the beat of it. Face-to-face with a man said to be her future husband, white-knuckled, she fought for control. *Mother is angry, yes. Of course, I knew there would be consequences but I never expected this. To think my parents would betray me in such a way never once entered my mind.*

"Dear, please do not be rude. Give Mr. Kirby the courtesy of acknowledging his presence."

She lifted her trembling hand to his out-stretched palm. Her throat constricted, and she could not look directly at him. Instead, she focused on his gray pinstripe slacks and moved up inch by inch until she reached his handsome face. An explosion echoed in her head as his eyes penetrated her soul. He stood over six feet tall, solidly built, and she felt small in his presence. She was not sure what she had expected, wasn't sure she expected anything at all. A woodsy fragrance tickled her nose. Broad muscular shoulders complimented the rugged look, but at the same time exuded finesse, well-schooled manners, and proper decorum. His eyes were kind and compassionate, and her hand fit in his warm grasp like a comfortable glove.

"It's so nice to meet you, Miss Squire. My mother and I are well versed in all of your fine accomplishments. Your parents are proud, indeed." His speech was polished, controlled, and proper, yet his voice remained soft. His gaze rendered her speechless—a prisoner.

"I apologize Mr. Kirby, Ruthie is usually so glib and never this unpleasant. I cannot imagine why she's acting this way."

Startled by a sharp pinch on the back of one arm, she managed to disengage from his grasp and motioned for him to sit. She cleared her throat. "Pardon me, Mr. Kirby, please forgive me. Won't you sit over here?" She indicated the gold velvet settee he had occupied a moment ago and watched his movements as he followed her direction. *Muscular thighs…he does not make his living behind a desk. He moves with such purpose and the way he sits—elbows resting on his knees, large hands holding his hat, he…*Flushed and embarrassed, she took her seat beside him and hoped her expression did not give way to the thoughts crossing her mind.

The two-story brownstone had been Ruth's home from the day of her birth, a sanctuary from the modern upside-down world of 1929 in Detroit, Michigan. Until recently, she had loved this warm, relaxed house and appreciated her mother's lavish taste. Now, it had turned into a guardhouse, and she yearned for freedom and independence. Last night, an eternity ago, her rebellion triggered this situation, and Peter Kirby appeared. She knew Mother, who now occupied the single chair in the room, leaving Father to stand by the fireplace, chose the parlor for this rendezvous because of its intimate arrangement.

"Ruth is a lovely name," Peter said. "Are you named for your beautiful mother, Miss Squire?" Peter moved a bit closer and touched her hand.

Mother laughed aloud, "Why no, but thank you, Peter. May I call you Peter?" Mrs. Squire flirted, unabashed. "I chose Ruth's name from the Bible. It fits her, don't you think?"

"Indeed it does, Mrs. Squire." Peter addressed the older woman, but his attention remained riveted on her.

Why won't he look away? He never wavers. I must look away. She couldn't.

"Our marriage is in a fortnight, Miss Squire. Do you have any questions for me? I know this is sudden. I want to make this as pleasant as possible." His hand now covered hers.

"Oh, I think we know as much as we need to know, Peter. Your mother gave us a detailed profile of your life. We are happy with our choice." Mother rose to pour tea and handed a fragile china cup to the hopeful bridegroom.

Peter shifted his gaze from Ruth…slowly. "I am sure you have all the answers you need, Mrs. Squire. However, Ruth is the one who must commit. Surely, she has a few questions." He looked steadfast into the eyes of the matron this time.

Ruth's heart skipped and the silence took on a life of its own. *Such boldness, how will she react? No one ever talked to Mother in that tone.* She stole a glance, but turned back to look again on the man who dared such effrontery.

His rugged face glowed bronze in contrast to his white blond hair, and the blue in his eyes had turned to ice

Mother was the first to look away.

Peter accepted the teacup and turned back to Ruth. "Do you have any questions for me, Miss Squire?"

Questions, of course I have questions. The only one she could think of flew out of her mouth before she knew it. "How old are you, Mr. Kirby?"

"I am twenty-seven. I know you think it is a lot older, but it is a bonus for a young woman in this modern time. I am already established. You will want for nothing."

Gosh, he doesn't look almost thirty.

"You will meet my mother tomorrow," Peter said. "You'll like her, I think. She is an accomplished woman, as Mrs. Squire well knows. I am sure you will have had time to think of more questions when we return. I must take my leave I'm afraid. I have a route to run which requires an early start. I will be here, as well, tomorrow so I will see you again. I hope this hasn't been altogether distasteful for you." He patted her hand and stood to leave.

From her vantage point, he towered over her. She rose, determined not to look him in the eye, and managed a curt nod. Both parents escorted him out of the room. The front door closed and she waited, fists clenched by her side, jaw set. *I'll have MY say now.*

Minutes passed; the grandfather clock in the corner ticked louder, and still Mother did not return.

"She's not coming. Coward."

She swept the skirt of her gown high and stomped up the stairs, back to her room. Once inside, she collapsed on the bed. The willow green floral comforter muffled the sobs. "How could one little escapade end like this? Can they force me to marry this man? How long have they known him and where does he come from? I know all my parents friends, and I have never seen him before."

◆◆◆◆

Priscilla Squire knew Ruth would wait in the parlor to confront her and decided not to play into her hand. The kitchen was empty, the cook already gone for the day. The evening meal's aroma of roast beef mixed with the robust fragrance of coffee lingered in the air. She opened the drawer of the polished light oak buffet, drew out her personal stationery, settled herself at the kitchen table, and composed a note to her errant daughter. She rang the velvet bell rope in the corner to summon Sarah. The maid appeared immediately.

"Take this to Ruth and be quick about it. I need you to help me pack," she ordered. "And Sarah…"

"Yes, ma'am?"

"Lock her door as you leave. Bring me the key."

The room dimmed to dark, but Priscilla sat down at the table and lowered her face into her hands. "I am doing the right thing. I know I am. It is what I must do. Robert does not understand our dire predicament. His writing doesn't sell any more and he is out of touch, such a stubborn man. Once more, I am left to make the impossible decision." She sighed, straightened her voluminous skirts, and exited the kitchen.

At Ruth's bedroom door, she stopped to listen. The loud sobs tore at her heart, but she forced herself to ignore them and continue down the hall to her own room.

Sarah already stood at the closet door, one hand poised above the clear glass knob.

Priscilla hurried to block the door. "I will get that, Sarah. You go to Mr. Squire's room and get his clothes ready."

"But the luggage is cumbersome, madam."

"Do as I say Sarah. I said I would handle it."

Sarah curtsied, held out the key to Ruth's room, and left.

A quick turn of her wrist locked the closet door. She slipped the key ring back in her pocket and lowered herself onto the blue velvet vanity bench. Practiced fingers removed the pins from her long, steel-gray hair, and it fell to her shoulders. She stared into the Queen Anne mirror. "I almost made the wrong choice when I was a girl. I will not let the same happen to Ruth.

◆◆◆◆

After a time, the tears subsided, and Ruth lay silent on the rumpled bed, her room a safe haven. Light from the gas street lamp filtered through the creamy lace curtains and gave the soft rose and willow green décor a cheery ambience, which did not match her mood. She sat up, pulled both knees to her chin, and hugged them close.

"They cannot be serious. Marriage—for a few minor infractions of the rules? Mother is stern, but not cruel. It's a test. That has to be it. They want to show me what they could do if I don't straighten up. Okay, I have learned my lesson. I'll show them."

A knock on the door interrupted her thoughts. "Miss Ruthie, may I come in?" She opened the door.

Sarah stood in the hall. "Your mother left you a note."

"Am I off the hook? Did they change their minds?"

Sarah shook her head, adjusted her white cap, and left her to read it alone.

Dear daughter, we know this is a great shock to you, but trust you will understand we only serve your best interests. We have arranged a trip by train to New York where we will assemble your wedding trousseau. Mrs. Kirby will call on you, with Peter, on the morrow. Sarah will attend in our absence. Wear the green again. Mr. Kirby barely saw it, and his mother will love you in it. Present yourself well and we will see you in a few days.

Mother and Father.

Her hand crumpled the note, and she hurled it across the room. In the silence, she heard voices outside in the alley. She pulled back the curtain, surprised to see Peter standing beside the milk wagon, talking to Father. A moment later, he waved to him and climbed to his perch atop the truck.

I must admit he is a fine figure of a man. Chills rippled through her body, and she tried to shake off the odd sensation in her stomach. "That is the point. He's a man! I'm a girl, not a woman. I have never had a proper boyfriend, and I am to marry a milkman? I must get out of here."

She ran to the door and tried the knob. *Locked again. Sarah must have turned the key when she left*. Panic crept up her spine, and she whirled around. The oval mirror atop the dressing table reflected disheveled black hair, alabaster skin as pale as the moon, and round, frightened dark eyes. She looked to the window again, as a means of escape. Her fingers dug into the sash. It would not budge, no matter how hard she pushed. Shiny, new penny nails forced deep in the wood sealed her prison. Tears filled her eyes.

Chapter Three

Peter took his time on the way home from the Squires' to digest the day's events. Earlier this morning, he was surprised when he eased open the back door of the small cottage and tiptoed into the tidy kitchen, a mixed bouquet of flowers sequestered safely behind his back. Seldom could he afford a surprise for his mother, and he knew she would scold him for such an extravagance, but he could not suppress a bit of a smile. He had picked up three more clients on his milk run, the horses were strong and healthy, and he had clinched top driver of the month. Times were good, and Mother deserved something bright in her life. After all, raising his two younger brothers alone took every ounce of energy she could muster. He heard her soft voice in the parlor. Careful not to frighten her, he hesitated outside the wide archway. What he heard would turn his world upside down.

"Yes, Mrs. Squire, I am ready to seal the agreement. Don't worry about my son. I will convince him. The marriage can take place as you wish. Ruth is a lovely girl and a perfect match for my son."

The beautiful bouquet landed in a tattered heap on the floor. "Mother?"

Elizabeth Kirby turned. "Why Peter, you're home early. I have the most wonderful news." She returned the telephone to the cradle and hurried to embrace him.

He escaped her outstretched arms. "What do you mean about an arrangement of marriage?"

"Son, you know I want the best for you. I have discussed this at length with the Squires, and I believe this girl is perfect for you."

He paused and took a ragged breath. "I am not interested in marriage. I'm not ready. The business is only beginning and I have you and the boys to care for. I am not equipped to take on a wife."

"On the contrary, you need a wife. The boys are a handful for me now that papa is gone. It is my wish to see you happily married and stable. Think of the help she would be to all of us. You are to meet her this evening, dear. If perchance you do not fancy her, we will reconsider. My intuition is right on this, please trust me." She laid a hand on Peter's arm. "Give it a chance. That is all I ask."

He paced the length of the room, fists flexing, open, closed, and open. "All right, if I don't like her, you will not hold me to it?"

"Certainly not. I do want your happiness, Peter. I will have your good suit ready when you get home. You're to call on her at six."

But, he did like her, much more than he thought he would. He continued the drive home in silence, the clop of the horse's hooves on the cobblestone soothing his jangled nerves. "She didn't like me and must think I am a buffoon. Her mother did not give her beauty justice…she is exquisite. Of course, why would she want the likes of me? How could I be so stupid? What a terrible idea."

The clear night and bright stars did nothing to lift his heavy heart. Unusual hardship followed the family since they moved to this country. To the exclusion of his own welfare, his mother and brothers became his primary concern. Father died penniless, in debt, and Peter worked hard to pay off the extra bills. The mourning period stretched endless for Mother. Wife to John Kirby for 40 years, she knew nothing else. Lost, lonely, with no means of income, she sank into despair. College plans to study business disappeared in the wake of his father's death. His two young brothers presented added problems for his mother. His hopes of a higher education dashed, he took a bold step and moved the clan to the United States.

The decision proved the right one. Mother's cheeks showed new color and the boys blossomed. Unfortunately, for him, Mother took on a new project, a wife for her oldest son. His loneliness never came to the surface until Mother mentioned it. "What should I tell her, now? How can I tell her the young woman did not like me? She will be upset and try to find another one. Ruth is a beautiful woman, creamy white skin, shiny black hair. Mother is excited about the meeting tomorrow, although I have reservations."

The horses, Patch and Bunny, nickered as if to join the one-sided conversation. "Ruth looked very upset. Mrs. Squire convinced me her daughter knew about the arrangement, but the visit surprised her, I know. I acted too eager. I should have stood up instead of rushing over there. I have so little experience with women. Maybe I don't need a wife, anyway. There is my milk business to run, people who depend on me. I have no time for marriage. Say, get up, Patch, what are you doing? Oh, sorry old boy—we're home already." He could see the shadow of his mother in the window of their small cottage home. "She is eager to hear all about it, isn't she Sally?" The second horse threw her head up and down as if in agreement.

Mother met him at the door. "Well, is she simply beautiful? She *is* attractive isn't she, Peter? Goodness knows you deserve the most beautiful woman in Detroit. So tell me what happened?"

"Mother calm down, I will answer all your questions. Let me in the door first. Is supper ready? Where are the boys?"

"Of course, let me take your coat. Here, sit down, and I will put supper on the table. I fed your brothers earlier so we could talk in private. You know how they are, curious little knuckleheads full of questions."

"Not like you, right Mother?" He took a big bite of roast beef, chewed slowly, and watched her in amusement.

"Peter, please, don't tease me. If she isn't the right woman, we will find another."

"She is beautiful, Mother. Let me finish dinner, and we can talk in the parlor. There is a small problem."

The small, cozy cottage met the basic needs all the income from his milk delivery business could afford. Everything they had tucked away bought the wagon and horses to start over in America. Mother brought her most meaningful items to this new country and turned the parlor into a replica of the one in Holland. Handmade lace doilies covered the overstuffed chairs and settee like snowcaps on a winter morning. Matching lace dressed the windows. Her lifetime collection of antique figurines filled the room, cherubs, dancing ladies, tulips, horses and carousels. Her father created one-of-a-kind porcelain figurines, his life's work, and his artisanship became renowned in the homeland. Peter refused to allow her to sell them after his father died and vowed she would never lose the priceless treasure.

Tea trickled into the fragile china teacups of her famous collection. He always thought his calloused fingers would break one of the dainty cups. Nevertheless, Mother insisted they continue the old customs. "Our meeting is at teatime tomorrow," he said.

"Lovely. You did not mention the Squires. Will they attend?" She sat on the edge of her favorite chair, back straight and dress folded properly around her ankles.

Peter admired her effort to retain traditional manners and decorum. He prized her blonde tresses, swept demurely into the fashionable chignon of the day. Still a handsome woman, the soft blue, homespun dress brought out her blue eyes. "Her parents left for New York to acquire the trousseau. The maid will stand in as chaperone. Are you sure we should do this Mother? We do not know her, and I might botch the whole thing because I have no experience."

Peter's mother set her teacup on the lamp table. "You are a Kirby, Peter. You have natural charm and charisma like your father. She is lucky to have you. Now tell me about your future wife, dear."

They talked about the upcoming events until his bone-tired body gave up, and he excused himself.

"We have an exciting day ahead, Peter. Get some rest."

◆◆◆◆

Peter ripped the shirt from his torso and threw it on the bed. "Rest…indeed! Sleep, when all I see are the chocolate pools of her eyes, the curve of her cheek, those plump, succulent red lips."

The bed groaned under his weight. He bowed his head and entwined his fingers in his hair. "I was fine until Mother made a mission to marry me off. I didn't need women in my life until now. It never occurred to me my body would betray me like this. I can't stop thinking about her. What kind of cad am I? I barely know her, yet the heat burns in my loins. Why couldn't Mother leave me alone? Now, I must endure the torture of the flesh." He lifted his head from his hands and there she stood, in the middle of the room, black hair disheveled, her sensuous smile said come-hither. The moonlight illuminated her gauzy white night dress and revealed a lithe figure.

He gasped. "What are you doing here?"

She reached toward him. "I want you, Peter. I wanted you from the first glimpse, but was afraid to let you know. Sleep wouldn't come. I had to see you, kiss you. Come to me Peter. Come."

The illusion dissolved the second he reached out to her. Moon dust filled his empty fist. The night tortured him, robbed him of sleep. Dreams of Ruth floated through his subconscious mind. He saw her laughing in the garden, give a coy look over her shoulder, and run behind a tree. He'd pretend to look for her, and when he found her their kisses burned hot.

He woke, sheets twisted around his sweat soaked body, and an ache in his heart. Only twenty-hours since he first laid eyes on his future wife and need consumed him.

The early morning sun made its entrance. Peter, wide awake, stared at the ceiling. "I don't know if I can see her today. She might reject me." He sat up. "I must call this off. I can't stand this torture."

The hot shower calmed his restlessness, and by the time he finished, knew he would not end the plan already in motion. He wanted her, and he would have her.

◆◆◆◆

A dreary rain drizzled lightly and cast a gloomy pallor on the morning.

"Oh, you look beautiful this morning, Ruthie. Your cheeks are pink, your eyes sparkle. Mr. Kirby's a lucky man, indeed."

"No matter, Sarah, I'll look like my mother after I am wed. Babies, drab days of nothing but mindless social gatherings, and household chores will steal my beauty soon enough. I want more, Sarah."

"We all be wantin' more, child. What we dream and how we end up are often two different things. You should be proud and thankful your parents watch out for you and give you a stable life, not actin' like a spoiled, willful child. Wish I had parents who cared so much for me."

"I know Father spoils me, but Mother's sternness balances it all. I do know they love me. But to arrange a marriage because I sneaked out the window is going too far. Can't you talk to them for me, Sarah?"

"Oh, to be sure, tell my employer how to raise his daughter, a wise choice indeed for future employment. Enough talk. When Mrs. Kirby and

Peter arrive, I'll come fetch you. Mind you watch your tongue and stay civil, or something worse might happen to you."

She waited in silence, hands in her lap, and looked around the room. *It could be the last time I see my lovely room.*

A soft knock roused her from melancholy. "Come in Sarah."

◆◆◆◆

Ruth stood like a statue at the parlor door, dreamlike. Two days ago, she and Ginny planned a schoolgirl's adventure, and today her fiancé's mother sat in the next room. How in the world did this happen?

Sarah reached for the door handle, but Ruth intercepted. A silent, pleading look implored the maid to end the charade. Instead, Sarah shook her head and walked through the door.

"Mrs. Kirby, Peter. Welcome." Sarah began.

Peter rose, removed his hat, and bowed. "May I present my mother, Elizabeth Kirby."

Sarah curtseyed and turned to present Ruthie. "This is Ruth Squire, daughter of Priscilla and Robert Squire. Ruth, please meet Elizabeth Kirby."

She gathered her courage, fought the urge to bolt and run, and curtseyed to the older woman. "I am pleased to meet you, Mrs. Kirby." As an afterthought, she turned to Peter and said, "Mr. Kirby." Ruth took the chair opposite her guests.

After an awkward silence, Mrs. Kirby took up the conversation. "So tell us, Ruth. Have you graduated high school yet?"

Fascinated by the stylish woman, she hesitated. "Why, I don't graduate until the spring, Mrs. Kirby. I must say, your dress is lovely. The color is most unusual. Is it the new fashion this year?"

"Oh, my no, child. I brought this dress from the homeland. It is my favorite color. My dear husband bought it in France. The color is *wild blush*. A daring name I suppose, but fitting. Your emerald dress is lovely against your skin, dear. I use to have skin like yours…when I was young."

"May I ask after your husband, Mrs. Kirby?" The blush rose to Ruth's cheeks as she realized the question might be inappropriate.

"We lost Mr. Kirby two years ago. My son Peter brought us here to start a new life. Oh good, here's the tea."

Sarah set the laden tray on the table beside the settee and began to pour the steaming liquid. She reached for the plate of scones and offered them to the guests.

"Oh, no, just tea, thank you. I couldn't eat," Peter said.

"Sarah makes the flakiest scones around, Mr. Kirby. I wouldn't want to offend her if I were you." Ruth smiled and took the tray from Sarah.

"Peter, you should try these. They are wonderful. I must have the recipe."

Peter accepted the scone. "Of course, pardon me Sarah. I thought I'd make a mess of it and look a bit foolish. I love scones, thank you."

"Ruth, my dear, I have planned a trip to town tomorrow to shop. Would you like to go? I would love to have the companionship of such a stylish young lady. A fresh look so to speak. Sarah, would you have any objection?"

"I don't know, Mrs. Kirby. I would hate to go against Mrs. Squire's instructions."

"I will take full responsibility, don't worry." Elizabeth smiled at her. "Is there anyone you would like to invite along, Ruth? We could make a day of it. A girlfriend, perhaps?"

"Oh, Mrs. Kirby, it does sound delightful. Could I ask my best friend, Ginny?" She glanced at Sarah for a brief instant.

"Of course, how lovely, I will look forward to meeting her. Now, Peter, I am going to have a word with Sarah. She needs to give me the scone recipe. Would you engage Miss Squire in conversation while I am occupied?"

"Of course, Mother. Do hurry though; I fear it is going to rain. I wouldn't want to get caught in a storm on the way home." After the two women left, Peter spoke first.

"Miss Ruth, may I be so bold to speak frankly? You are surprised by all this, aren't you? Did your parents not tell you of their plans?"

"No, they did not. I hadn't a clue until I met you last night. I apologize for my rudeness yesterday, but you have to know, I don't want to marry. I want to see the world. My parents have other plans for me because I sneaked out a window yesterday." She looked up and spoke boldly. Maybe her honesty would deter him.

"I see. You are an unwilling participant. It makes it much more difficult to woo you. You are a beautiful woman, Ruth, a prize for any man. I might not be what you aspire for, but I own my own business and do very well. I could take care of you," he said. "Mother will be so disappointed. I can imagine the parade of girls she will put before me." He looked up quickly. "Pardon me, Miss Squire. Of course, this is not about me, it's about you. I am afraid I thought aloud. Please forgive me."

"Mr. Kirby, you are a fine-looking man. That's not the problem. I want to *do* things, see the world. Please understand. I am not ready."

Peter raised the teacup to his lips. "Certainly, I would not want to marry you against your will, but your parents are hell-bent to have us wed. My mother, too. What shall we do? You can't run away. They made it very clear last night the arrangements are made and an agreement struck between my mother and your parents."

She sighed. "I know, Mr. Kirby. I'm still thinking of a plan."

"Please, call me Peter. After all, we are in this together. I have no reservations about marriage to you, you know. I would be honored to have you as my wife. Can we go through the motions for right now, please our parents, and see how things go? What do you say? It has buoyed Mother's spirits after the sadness of the last two years. My happiness is her sole focus right now."

"Doesn't an arranged marriage seem wrong to you, Peter? Don't you believe in love? *Real* love? Don't you want to fall in love?" she pleaded.

Peter hung his head. "My mother and father's marriage was arranged, Ruth. I never knew a day when their love wasn't strong."

Her mouth fell open in disbelief.

"You see, if it worked for my parents, I hoped it would work for me. Mother's instincts are good when it comes to people. I trust her."

"Well, she is wrong in this case. I am wild, uncontrollable. I do not like rules. I will be a hindrance to you. Marriage may look attractive to you from your parent's point of view, but I am a different breed. I'll make your life miserable."

Peter looked up. "I will take my chances, Ruth. I want this to happen. Won't you go along for awhile? It won't happen right away. We could ask to postpone it for a bit. Grant me this one favor. Please."

She didn't answer. Her plan had failed.

Elizabeth Kirby swept into the room. "What have you two young people been talking about?"

"The weather mostly, Mother. I am not sure a trip to town is a good idea tomorrow. It looks as though it might be a wet day."

"A little rain won't hurt anything, will it, Ruth?"

"I suppose not, Mrs. Kirby. It *will* be good to get out of this house for a spell."

Elizabeth stood. "Come, Son. We should let this dear girl rest for the afternoon. I intend to keep her very busy tomorrow. It is so lovely to meet you, Ruth. I look forward to tomorrow morning. Is eleven o'clock all right? We can do lunch in town."

"Certainly, Mrs. Kirby. I will get a message to Ginny."

Peter rose, took Ruth's hand, and raised it to his lips. "It was a pleasant visit. I look forward to the next."

The door closed and she heard a giggle behind her. She turned to see Sarah, arms akimbo and a big smile on her face. "Is it a blush I'd be seein' on your cheeks? You did like him, then?"

"Forget it Sarah, you are not going to convince me." She ran up stairs, anxious for the sanctuary of her room. She didn't know what she felt. He *is* kind, good-looking, and his mother warm and friendly. It still does not change anything. It could be an act. He might be a mean, cantankerous, evil beast. One meeting did not prove anything.

Still, her heart beat fast and butterflies whirled in her stomach. *It's fear and confusion, that's all.* The reflection in the mirror confirmed the blush. Her hair, a bit ruffled, created a sultry look, the image of a virtual stranger. She shook herself and went to the door. "I must get in touch with Ginny. I cannot wait to get out of this house! I'll try Father's study again."

She tiptoed down the stairs and tried the door. It opened with ease. There, on the old desk, stood the candlestick telephone. She started to dial the operator when Sarah burst in.

"What are ya doin', Ruth? You're not to use the telephone, and you know your father's study is forbidden when he is not here."

"I'm going to ring Ginny and tell her about our shopping trip tomorrow. Surely you can't object to that."

Sarah stood silent and frowned. "My, and the wrong decision could get me fired. An idea is a-comin' to me. I need to go to the market for tonight's meal. I might be willin' to run by her house and deliver the message m'self. If you use the telephone, Nellie will tell your folks. You cannot trust that busy-body operator."

"Oh, Sarah, what a capital idea. Are you leaving now?" She rested the earpiece back in the cradle. Eager to have the house to herself, she grabbed Sarah's hands and turned her around twice.

Sarah jerked her hands free and placed them on her hips. "You are a bit eager to have me gone. What do ya have up your sleeve, missy?"

Ruth struck a pose, the back of one hand against her mouth, eyes wide. "Why Sarah, I have nothing up my sleeve. You don't trust me…when we have been friends so long?"

The housekeeper laughed aloud. "It is *because* I have known ya so long that I don't trust a single hair on yer head. I'll be leavin' directly. Mind you behave yourself while I am gone."

Ruth shut the door to the study and meandered around the house for a few minutes. *I wonder if I will enjoy this warm home for much longer, or will I leave it for another soon?* Her wanderings led her to the kitchen where she had taken many a meal with only Sarah and occasionally their gardener, Oscar. She loved sitting at the butcher-block table while eating a hearty breakfast of bacon, eggs, and Sarah's wonderful blueberry muffins. Laughter echoed through the kitchen when Oscar shared stories of how her mother considered herself a master gardener. He told of his displeasure at her interference in the roses, and how he went back to restore the damage Mrs. Squire did to the garden. His thick, black eyebrows and mustache covered a kindly face. A stout, round man, his agility in the garden always surprised Ruth. The flowers became the pride of the neighborhood, and Mrs. Squire took a lot of the credit, much to Oscar's dismay. "How many more times will I enjoy the easy banter, unbridled by proper manners and decorum? This is my true home, right here in this kitchen."

Before she realized it, she stood in front of the parlor. Peter's face drifted into her mind, and the heat of the memory rose to her cheeks. Angry and confused at the sudden surge of desire, she bounded up the stairs to watch out the window for Sarah to leave. "Finally." The curtain fell back into place, and she raced down the hall to her mother's room.

"They wouldn't nail *all* the windows shut." She opened the door. "It *still* smells of violets in here. Maybe I can get the window open." In three strides, she crossed the room and grabbed the window sash. "Oh fudge, no luck. Now what?" Her leg bumped the dressing table and rattled the perfume bottles. "What does Mother do with all these perfumes? Every bottle and atomizer is different, elegant, and feminine, so unlike her." She surveyed the room for more insights. *The closet!*

"Now is as good a time as any." The glass doorknob beckoned to her, a forgotten fancy brought once more to light. She placed her hand on the knob and turned. "Locked." A wooden coat rack stood in the corner nearest the door, an old, faded dress hung lifeless on the tree. She rummaged her hand in the pocket. "Eureka! Now let's see if it is the right one."

The long key slid in easily, and she smiled at the click when the lock sprung. She stepped into the roomy wardrobe and stared at the neat rows of gray and black dresses displayed like soldiers, perfectly aligned. On the floor, in consummate formation, sat sturdy, sensible shoes—all black. Nothing pretty, nothing fancy. She noticed a lingering scent in the closet, something curious. The forbidden vault showed nothing of interest, however. She started to turn around, but something shiny caught her eye in the deep recesses of the small room.

The dresses whispered as she made her way past them—she ignored their complaints. The closet went on forever. When she thought the end near, it turned a corner. She paused, tempted to venture on, bewitched by an unusual sight. A bracelet sat like a sentry atop a glass shelf attached to the far wall. Three strands of diamonds sparkled, set alight from the open door's illumination. She reached out to touch them, one hand poised above the radiant stones. Instead, she drew back, conquered by curiosity and the unknown room ahead. She followed the turn and caught her breath.

A rack stood, out of sight, full of fancy gowns, all colors, and styles. Beautiful ballroom dresses, an array of ruffles and flounces, plunging necklines, feathers and boas, purple, red, bright blue, yellow, tangerine. Shoes lined up under each dress and matched perfectly the color of the gown. Above the clothes, shelves of beautiful long gloves, diamond tiaras, and overstuffed jewelry boxes displayed necklaces, bracelets, and earbobs. She couldn't breathe, couldn't comprehend her mother owned such opulent attire, much less wore it. She touched the silky fabrics and reveled in the extravagant softness. "Why did Mother hide all this from me? Why doesn't she wear these things? In all of my seventeen years, I've never seen her in any of these clothes. Not one piece of jewelry."

A musty perfume emanated from the clothes, and the air became heavy and pungent in the small space. A dark, heavy curtain hung at the end of the row. She pushed it aside to reveal a beautiful white vanity. *My goodness, a surprise around every corner.* Suddenly, the room closed in on her. "I'm dizzy. My head is spinning. It must be the stale perfume. Maybe if I rest for a moment…"

She eased herself down on the white velveteen bench and closed her eyes. In the deep, emotional exhaustion of her mind, voices penetrated the foggy slumber. No matter how hard she tried, her eyes wouldn't open, and she slipped deeper into the black hole of exhaustion. In the misty regions of her mind, she thought she heard voices.

"Sarah, do you think the waist is right? There is a slight pucker. I cannot have a pucker in my party dress. Snooty Sylvia Arnold would have a snide remark or two, to be sure."

"Priscilla Williams, if you would stand still for one minute I can make the adjustment. All this wigglin' will just not do!"

Sarah? When did she get back from the market? Priscilla Williams? We have a guest? Priscilla is Mother's name. Ruth struggled to make sense of the voices.

"Oh, pooh, Sarah, you're an old fuddy duddy. Do you think rose is the right color for me? Maybe it's too soft. The boys might not notice me. I should wear red. What do you think?"

"I already told you, you're not listenin'. Now be still."

"But, red is my color. You know it looks dramatic against my gorgeous black hair."

"We don't have time to fit another dress, Missy. The ball is tomorrow night. And ya know your mother doesn't want you to wear the loud color. It's not becomin' for a young debutante. Too garish. Besides, I need to finish this tonight. We have the ribbons to choose for your hair and the jewels to compliment the dress. What shoes will you wear? There are a million details yet to go over. Drat, I have run out of thread. Don't move while I run up to my room and fetch another spool."

Ruth managed to open one eye, just a slit. The crack between the door and the frame showed light from the guest room, and shadows danced in front of her, sparking her imagination and a scene in her mind. The flamboyant young lady preened in front of the full length mirror, turned her head this way and the other. Black hair bounced across her shoulders. She pulled up the hem of the dress and giggled when she revealed a slim, white ankle. An exaggerated curtsey followed. "Why thank you, Master Richard. I would love to dance the waltz with you." She pulled her shiny hair atop her head and examined the effect.

She is a vain one, for sure.

Sarah returned and continued to pull and sew to get the right fit. Miss Williams pouted in the mirror, posing.

"Breakfast's ready soon, child. You must eat and get some rest so the dark circles don't settle under your eyes."

"I'm too excited to sleep. I wonder if the handsome Richard Charmain will grace the party tomorrow night. I would love to dance with *him*."

The beautiful Miss Williams let the dress fall to the floor, and Sarah gathered it into her arms, headed for the closet.

Ruthie gasped at the old-fashioned undergarments the woman wore—bloomers and a corset. *Oh, it must be a costume party, that's it. A beautiful lady wouldn't wear those outdated things on a normal day.* Hidden behind the vanity she felt safe from discovery and thought she heard the hanger squeak across the bar. The door closed, moments passed, and the voices ceased. She struggled to her feet and shook her head in an effort to clear the drugged feeling. *Did I imagine the whole thing?* Dizzy, she held on to the vanity to steady herself, but her hand slipped, and she grabbed the corner.

The edge of a half-open drawer stabbed her finger. She looked down. A red satin ribbon dangled lazily over the side. Unable to resist the temptation, she pulled the drawer open. "Letters?" One by one, she thumbed through the envelopes. They all had the same name written in a fine female script, **Captain Alexander Adams.** "Who is Captain Adams?" She glanced around the small coatroom as if someone would come out of the dark recesses and catch her. Finally, she opened the top one. Dated almost twenty years ago, it read…

My Dear Captain, I remain distraught. I am to marry Robert Squire. My soul is wounded, my spirit destroyed. I thought you might call upon me and make your love known. I wait to hear from you and make an honest woman of me. My thoughts are only of you.

Always yours,
Priscilla Squire

Chapter Four

Banker Eric Horton admired his likeness in the cherry-finished floor mirror in the bedroom of his childhood home, long past its prime. A lifelong bachelor, the décor lacked any hint of a female touch. Dark wood and dreary curtains, threadbare and ancient, left the chamber cold and colorless. The room echoed at the snap of his gold-plated pocket watch. "This evening I will make my intentions known to Mrs. Squire. I have maneuvered her thus far and now, she can't deny me. It won't be long before I will insure my standing in this community with the introduction of a new wife, which will secure my promotion to bank president. They can't say no if I have the required family already in place."

He put the watch back into his waistcoat, straightened his brocade vest, and slicked back his thin, black hair. "Manson, have Audie bring the car around. I am going out this evening."

The stooped-shouldered, white haired butler entered the room with Eric's black suit jacket. "Should I help you with this first, Master Eric?"

"No, I can manage. Get the car."

"Right away, sir."

Eric preened like a peacock in the mirror, his prominent stomach sucked in to better show off his profile. The back of his left hand patted the jowls of an abundant chin. He chose to ignore the cartoon like appearance of his hawk-like nose. "Not a bad catch, if I do say so, at forty-five years old. Any young woman would be delighted to bag me as a husband." He shut the bedroom door and whistled as he hurried down the stairs and out the front door.

The butler closed the door on the new ForDor Sedan, and Eric instructed his driver to head for the Squires' address on the wrong side of Woodward Avenue. He enjoyed the envious looks on his clients' faces when the sleek, black automobile arrived in front of their humble homes. It gave him great pleasure to know they could never own such a vehicle.

The brass knocker reverberated in the clear, star-filled night, and he thought the Squires might not be at home after all, though lights shown through the curtains. He had almost given up when the door opened a crack, and Sarah peeked out.

"May I help you, sir?" she asked.

"Yes, I am here to speak to the Squires, Miss. Tell them it is Eric Horton from the bank."

"I'm sorry. They aren't here. They went to New York for a few days. May I take your card? I will let them know you called." She stuck her hand out the door.

"Oh, of course, not home. I see. Well, yes. Here's my card." He flinched at the abrupt way Sarah snatched the document. The closed door mocked him as he realized it slammed in his face. He straightened his jacket and turned toward the car.

On the ride back to his home, he muttered aloud, "Just a minor setback. I can wait a few more days. It will be better anyway, put them deeper into my debt."

"Did you say something, sir? No problems, I trust." Audie addressed Horton as he rounded the corner.

"None you can help me with, I fear, only the same ignorant, puffed-up arrogance of the lower class. It's very wearisome." Horton knew he could trust his driver of many years, but all in all he too was of the lower class. Still…it was nice to rely on his loyalty.

Eric found solace in the library, another dark, gloomy room in the house. He detested the place, and it irked him he could not afford to move into a newer house in the more affluent district of town. "It was all right for my poor parents, but I am made of more extravagant fiber. It will bring a tidy sum from an unsuspecting young couple, and I already have someone in mind."

A knock interrupted his musing. "Yes, Manson. What is it?"

"Your evening cognac, sir," he replied.

"Yes, yes. Set it down on the desk. That will be all tonight, Manson. I have plans to make."

The butler placed the silver tray with the lone snifter of cognac on the desk, bowed, and left the room.

"I never thought to ask if they took Ruth with them. What in the world would they need in New York? Moreover, how could they afford the trip? They are in the throes of bankruptcy, thanks to me." He lifted himself from the chair, grasped the snifter in his hand, and inhaled the robust aroma of the golden brandy in a grand amateurish manner. "All my hard work is about to afford me the status to which I am entitled. Yes, I can wait a few days to issue the ultimatum."

Pudgy, jewelry-encrusted fingers strummed the desk as he thought out the well-formed plan. In a sudden burst of energy, he took a piece of personal stationery and penned a letter. Under his elegant initials EH, on the parchment he began….

Dear Mr. & Mrs. Squire,

It is with regret I must inform you of the foreclosure of the mortgage on your home. As you know, I have made several attempts to collect the past three month's payments without success. I stopped by your house this evening to discuss the matter and found you not at home, but off to New York. For what, I can only imagine. It is imperative you contact me on your return. You have no more leeway. I can, however, offer you a way out of this unfortunate situation. You must act immediately. A week. No more. My number is on my card. I expect to hear from you at the earliest possible time.

Always your servant,

Eric Horton, Account Manager

♦♦♦♦

Ruth's hands trembled. The parchment fell to the floor. "Mother was in love with a Captain Adams? How can this be possible? Father…" She scooped up the letter and read it again. "What will I find in the other ones? Should I even read them? This is all too much. First, a strange lady in the guest room, and now I find Mother's old love letters? Surely, it can't be true. I must get out of here."

She slammed the letters back in the drawer and navigated through the closet maze, caressing the party dresses one last time. "I need to find out who the strange woman is, and I need to ask Sarah about Mother." Ruth hurried out of her mother's room, careful to leave no evidence of her clandestine trespass.

She hesitated at the guest room door, walked by, turned, and stood before the door once again. The knob didn't give, and she dropped her hand at the sound of steps on the stairs. Hands on her hips, Ruth stomped to the head of the stairs and issued her ultimatum. "Okay, enough of this cloak and dagger business. Who is the woman in the guest room and why is she here?"

An armful of laundry muffled Sarah's startled cry. "My and ya did frighten me, Miss Ruthie. What woman? What are you talkin' about? There's no one in the guest room."

Ruth could see Sarah's puzzled look.

"Come on. I'll show you." She pointed to the guest room door. "Go ahead, open it."

Sarah set down her basket and reached for the door. "Okay, I opened it. Now will you be tellin' me what I am supposed to be seein'?"

Ruth brushed past the housemaid. The room stood in perfect order. No clothes on the bed, no messy dressing table, and no young woman. The blue ruffles on the bedspread hung perfectly in place. No hairbrush, no perfumes, no hair ribbons, nothing to indicate anyone was there.

"Sarah, I swear. There *was* a woman in here just a moment ago. At least, I think so. There were clothes strewn over the bed, and the dressing table was cluttered with hairbrushes, ribbons, and such." She went to the closet and flung open the door to reveal the truth. Nothing—except empty hangers and a few old boxes.

"There were dresses, shoes, and jewelry. Where did it all go? I waited too long. You got rid of it. How did you know I was in there, Sarah? It must be you. You knew I was in there didn't you?"

A long, black cloak hung at the end of the closet. Ruth rushed forward and pushed aside the cloak to reveal the corner turn. Her heart beat faster as she followed it. Her mother's drab dresses and shoes hung as they had a moment ago.

"No! I know what I saw, those dresses were there." She ran out of the closet, into the hallway, and tore into the top-heavy laundry basket.

"You are overwrought, Ruthie." Sarah called to her. "What your parents sprung on ya messed up your head. Come out of there. I have the very thing to soothe you." Sarah put an arm around Ruth's shoulder, led her downstairs, and settled her at the kitchen table.

The aromatic herbal tea calmed Ruth's nerves, and she listened while Sarah went on about Ginny's excitement at the invitation Peter's mother extended.

"Does she think I forgive her for running out on me? I hope you told her I will get my revenge."

"You know she could have done nothin' else, Ruthie. Her parents are sometimes harsher than yours."

"I know. I hoped for a little support from my best friend, I guess."

"You can talk to her later, Ruth. Finish your tea, have your soup, and get some rest. You have a big day tomorrow."

She let Sarah help her upstairs and arrange a warm comforter over her weary body. She fell asleep instantly, exhausted. An hour later, the front door slammed, and she awoke, startled. The comforter fell to the floor as she scampered from the bed to the window.

What is Father's banker, Mr. Horton doing here this time of night? She stomped toward the door and found it locked. "Sarah. Sarah!" Balled fists pounded on the solid oak barrier. "You come here right now. I mean it. I will make your life miserable if you don't let me out." She beat harder. "I will scream all night if I have to. You better open the door."

The key turned in the lock, and the door opened. Ruth stopped her screams, stood back, and rubbed her sore fists. "Well, it's about time. How dare you lock me in again. Why was Mr. Horton here, what did he want?" she demanded.

The petite blonde maid's pretty face crumpled. Ruth observed the wrinkled, white uniform, her cuffs soiled, and the smell of bleach. A round, pillbox cap sat askew on her head.

"Miss Ruth, I'm not knowin' what he wanted. He asked to see your parents. I told him when they would be back, and he left. Please Miss Ruth; I'm not supposed to open your door until mornin'. I don't want to get fired. You were so upset. I didn't want you wanderin' around the house."

Ruth sat down on the bed, shoulders slumped. "Sarah, I won't get you in trouble. You are my only friend in this house. Will you please just talk to me…like we use to when I was small? I *need* you. My brain is going to explode. Can you be my friend tonight and not an employee?"

A tiny smile tweaked the corners of Sarah's mouth. "We did have some good times, didn't we Ruthie? It has been a lifetime since we laughed together, shared secrets. I swear there is a dark cloud hangin' over this house. I cannot remember the last time the whole family showed true happiness."

Sarah put her hand on her hip. "Would you like to come down to the kitchen and share a pot of warm cocoa with me? Promise you won't tell?"

Ruth jumped off the bed and hugged Sarah tight. "Oh, you are the *best*. I knew I could count on you."

They giggled together, arms entwined, and clattered down the stairs.

Embers glowed in the brick fireplace, the last hurrah of a long day. Sarah made the cocoa while Ruth sat at the worn, wooden kitchen table, and chattered about Mr. Horton.

Sarah stirred the pot in a slow rhythm, glanced at Ruth, and changed the subject. "Ruthie, what did you do *this* time to upset your mother so much? It must have been terrible bad for her to make you marry Mr. Kirby."

"Mother didn't tell you? Oh, of course, she didn't." She grinned at the maid." Do you want to hear the *whole* story?"

Sarah sat two, hot steamy mugs of hot chocolate on the table, slid into the chair next to her, and cupped her chin in one hand. "Yes, the whole story."

Ruth stood, went into a semi-crouch, raised both hands like claws, and in a low, dramatic voice, began her tale of woe.

Sarah giggled.

"Well, I dropped my new, black satin shoes from the second-story window ledge. Poof." She tapped the table softly. "Ginny held the ladder below and yelled, *Hey, watch where you are throwing things, Ruthie. Those shoes came close to my head. Hurry, I can't hold this ladder forever. Someone will see me. I might be your best friend, but I am not taking the rap for your great escape plan.* I balanced on one foot and wobbled in a precarious fashion. *Shh, someone will hear you, Ginny. Just hold it still. This isn't easy, you know. My fringe caught on the windowsill.* The ladder trembled, and I thought I was a goner." She shot furtive glances around the room in dramatic style.

Sarah rewarded her performance with a snicker. "I could see Ginny glance around, nervous someone would see us. I landed with a thump on both feet, safe and sound. Ginny looked splendid in her red dress. I doubted my choice of black, but she reassured me. *Oh, no. Black is so dramatic with your new bob. The dress is perfect. The boys will all want to dance with you.* She is a little jealous of me, you see. We are exact opposites. Ginny's blond hair and blue eyes give her an innocent flair. I'm a bit more dramatic, don't you think?" Ruth struck a pose, one hand on her hip. She danced about the kitchen. This was the Ruthie she wanted to be, carefree…happy-go-lucky.

Sarah snapped a towel at her. "Go on, silly girl. What happened after that? Did your mother catch you comin' down the ladder?" She shoved the mug of cocoa toward the storyteller.

Ruth settled herself in her chair and continued. "I slipped my shoes on, grabbed Ginny's hand, and raced down the alley beside the house. We laughed about dancing the Charleston with Will Johnson and stopped at the hedge to see if anyone was around. Then, we heard it." She stopped to sip her cocoa.

"Well, what was it Ruthie, don't stop now," Sarah said.

"Umm Hmm."

"That was it? Umm Hmm? Who was it?" Sarah asked.

"We stood statue-like, afraid to breathe. I thought I imagined it. I nudged Ginny. *What was that, Ginny? Is someone on the other side of the hedge?* Ginny didn't utter a sound. The leaves rustled, and a hand poked through the hedge…with a pair of garden shears."

Sarah let out her breath in a loud groan.

Ruth continued, "*Going somewhere, ladies*? We both screamed. *Mother, what are you doing in the garden at night?* She babbled something about lanterns and it being 1929, but my blood pounded so hard in my ears, I couldn't pay attention. Of course, she asked the question again. *What are you and Ginny doing dressed like that this time of night and where are you going?* I adjusted my black sequin headband while I tried to think of a good reason. *It's a party at Ginny's house. A…a slumber party. I knew you wouldn't let me go, so I decided to take advantage of my bedroom window. I* ***am*** *17 after all.* Ginny jabbed me in the ribs. *You attend* *slumber parties dressed for dancing?* Mother asked. I jabbed Ginny back. She confirmed my story and beat a swift retreat down the alleyway. The rest is history, Sarah. I have remained locked in my room ever since, except to meet Mr. Kirby."

"Oh, Miss Ruthie, you *do* have a way of tellin' a story. You should be an actress."

"I want to be an actress. Mother will hear none of it. Says I need to marry, raise a family. Phooey. I want to travel, see the world. I don't want to end up like *her*. She has done nothing, gone nowhere. I need excitement." Ruth stared into space for a moment, and tears splashed the table's surface.

Sarah reached across the table and laid her hand on Ruth's arm. "Oh miss, don't cry. It will be all right. Please, don't cry."

"I don't want to marry. Not now. They cannot make me, can they, Sarah? Tell me what *you* think of Mr. Kirby. You can be truthful with me."

"It's not my place to talk about family matters, Ruthie."

"Come on, you are a woman, same as me. You must have noticed if he is handsome or not. Did he spark your interest at all?"

"Why, I declare, you think he is fine-lookin', don't you?" Sarah poked her in the arm. "Come on. Tell me what you're thinkin'."

Ruth sighed. "Well, when I looked into his eyes, I felt my stomach flip-flop. Tanned, tall, strong. He is handsome, I guess. I felt odd when I stood by him—jittery, light-headed. What do you suppose it means?"

Sarah cleared the cups from the table, went to the sideboard, and washed the last of the day's dishes. "I think it means you find him desirable. Maybe it means marriage will not be so bad. Maybe your mother has the right idea, Ruthie. She has lived a long time, you know, might be a good idea to trust her judgment."

"But what of *my* dreams … travel, being an actress? Am I to give it up, to marry a milkman? I don't care if he *is* handsome, he might be mean, lock me in my room, starve me. I might have to have tons of babies."

"Ruthie, you do go on. It's late, Ruthie. You need to go back to your room. I made a promise to them, ya know. Please? Your parents would not hand you over to someone like that."

"Oh, wouldn't they, Sarah? What about Mother's secret lover? I found them, you know, the letters. Why should I listen to her when she has done nothing but lie to her own daughter and Father?"

The cup shattered on the floor when Sarah whirled from the sink. Sudsy bubbles flew helter-skelter in the air, but she only stood there, hands dripping, mouth open. "What do you know about any letters?"

"Don't look so surprised, you have known about them all along. I've read them, Sarah. I know all about Captain Adams." Ruth's chin jutted forward. The shock on the maid's face confirmed what she already knew. Mother had a secret past.

"Those letters were destroyed on her wedding day. She gave them to me herself. How could you know about those?"

"So, you admit it. You have been in on the lie from the beginning. Who is Miss Williams, Sarah? I heard her, too. If you don't tell me the whole story, I will tell Father and destroy this family."

"Miss Williams? There is no Miss Williams in the house, child. Don't you know? Your mother's maiden name was Williams. The woman you thought you heard was your own mother!"

Chapter Five

"Orange juice, Peter? I squeezed it fresh this morning."

"What? Oh yes, that would be nice, Mother."

"Distracted, son? I expect you have the jitters."

The gloomy, rainy day dampened Peter's spirits. He wished for a turbulent day of storms, thunder, and lightning, reason enough to cancel the day of shopping. It didn't go unnoticed fresh flowers adorned the breakfast table, or his brothers were gone to school. She dressed to perfection, and the glow on her face reflected real joy. His mother was on a mission, and he did not have the heart to disappoint her.

"I didn't sleep well. Too much on my mind, so much to think about and prepare. A wife is a great responsibility."

Elizabeth Kirby placed a hand on her son's shoulder. "It will be fine, Peter. She is a lovely girl. There aren't many options for women, you know. She *knows* it. When she weighs her choices, she will decide on you, be sure."

He turned and looked into her soft, cornflower eyes, her face framed in hair like spun silk, and smiled. Unlike most women, Peter knew his mother's mindset. She knew this union would be a marriage of convenience, where love played little part. He understood her need to keep the family intact and to carry on the traditions unique to the lineage of Kirby.

"Come. It's time to go. I don't want to keep Ruth waiting." She grabbed her fur-lined wrap and held it out for his assistance.

Mother and son drove in silence for a few miles. The smell of rain permeated the air, a wet shopping day for sure...but she was glad to have the automobile with a part-time driver for the excursion later.

"How did your conversation go while you were alone yesterday, dear?"

Peter hesitated, clicked to Patch, and fiddled with the reins. *Should he tell her the truth or not*? "Mother, she doesn't want to get married and did not know anything about the arrangement until last night. The Squires had not told her. I don't know if I can do this, under the circumstances. It seems so cruel of them."

"You can do it, son. She took a shine to me. Give me a little time, I will convince her." She patted his knee and smiled.

"All right, Mother. I'll give it a little time. But, if she still has second thoughts, the deal is off, okay?"

"Yes, dear, of course."

Peter knew Mother would work hard to make the match work, and he smiled to himself. Well, at least she had a project now. Something to occupy her time, keep her mind from the memories of her dead husband and all the loss they had suffered since his death. He didn't mind being the focus of her attention, right now. She was the light of his life. Without her, he could not accomplish anything.

The ride continued in silence. Peter wondered if his life would turn upside down.

◆◆◆◆

Sarah squawked all the way up the stairs, fighting the grip Ruth had on her hand.

"I don't want to hear it, Sarah. You know those dresses are there, the letters, the jewelry. How can I live in the house all these years and never find them?" Ruth drug her into the guest room and threw open the closet door. Empty. Nothing but a few coat hangers.

"What in blazes are you doing?" Sarah jerked her hand out of Ruth's grip.

"Where are they, Sarah? What did you do with the dresses and the jewelry?"

"Didn't you hear me, Ruth? It was a dream, your imagination. Miss Williams is your mother's maiden name. You *know* that. This whole thing is playing tricks with your mind. Those letters…you read them. It was too much for you."

Ruth collapsed on the chair next to the closet. weak in the knees. "What…what did you say? Mother's maiden name? Yes, I know it's Williams."

◆◆◆◆

A light rain peppered the early morning streets of Detroit. Ruth leaned against the glass of her bedroom window and willed the morning to move along at a faster pace. She tried to put the events of last night out of her mind. The prospect of a day in town, which also included her best friend, gave her hope.

She decided on a smart blue print and a solid navy cloak to ward off the rain. The reflection in the mirror revealed a spot on the front lapel. "Oh, no, I can't wear it like this." She opened the door and called for Sarah.

"I can get it out. It will take a bit of a soak, though," Sarah declared.

Ruth stamped her foot. "I don't have time, Sarah. Mrs. Kirby will arrive in a few minutes."

"I remember a smart, gray cloak in your mother's closet, Ruthie. Why don't you use it today? It will compliment your dress just fine. I think it's a bit thicker, too. Better to fend off the rain. I'll go fetch it."

Ruth reached out to stop the housekeeper. "Wait, I can get it Sarah. You need to be downstairs when the Kirbys arrive."

"Well…I don't know, Ruthie. You know your mother wouldn't want you in her room, and after the episode last night, I think it's not a good idea."

"You agreed, Sarah. The whole story…and I agreed to keep silent about Mother. Until they come back, I have free rein in this house. By the look of it, I will not live here much longer, and I do not want my last days to be behind a locked door. I'll fetch the cloak. I will only be a moment. Mother will never know."

"See that ya are, then. I'll be downstairs."

The same lilac scent lingered, the glass doorknob still glittered from the light in the window, and beckoned her to enter the forbidden closet. She crossed the room slowly, hesitant to enter, afraid of what she would find. She groped around for the dangling string attached to the lone bulb in the ceiling. Once illuminated, the closet took on a more normal atmosphere. The solemn dresses whispered as her shoulders brushed past, and an ominous chill raised goose bumps on her flesh. Frightened, she hurried to the end, reached for the cloak, and stopped cold. A single blue boa feather lay on the floor. Her hands trembled. She bent down and picked it up.

"How did this get here? The fancy dresses were gone. Sarah must have moved them. Too bad she didn't take a little more care. I will put *this* in her face, and she cannot deny it."

She deposited the feather in the pocket of her dress and turned the corner. She stood dumbfounded. "What in blazes?" In exactly the fashion she left them, hung all the beautiful dresses she had ogled over, the shoes, the gloves, the jewelry, everything. Static electricity crackled, and once again, the heavy perfumed air made her reel, and dizziness overtook her. *I must hurry, they will be here soon, cannot be sick now. I should remind Sarah to air out the closet. Uh, oh, my head…I need to sit for a moment.*

Sarah's voice penetrated the musky air. "Ruthie? Where are you? Come out of there this instant."

"Coming, Sarah." She ran to the front of the closet, pulled the light cord, and closed the door. The doorbell snapped her out of the confusion.

From the top of the stairway, Ruth squealed while she bounded down the steps, "Ginny! I thought I would never see you again. I'm so glad you are here."

"Why would you think that? Who is this woman taking us shopping? I must say I am surprised at the invitation. Did you get into trouble? What did your mother do?"

"Stop blabbering, girl. Come in the parlor, and I will tell you everything."

They scampered off, heads together, chattering like chipmunks.

Fifteen minutes later the doorbell rang again, and Sarah ushered Mrs. Kirby into the house.

The girls stopped to listen, held each other's hands, and stared into each other's eyes. They could see the new arrival through the open door. Her navy blue suit dress complimented her blue eyes and fair hair.

"Good morning, Sarah. Are our girls ready?"

"They are in the parlor, ma'am. Before you go in, I must tell you, I am a bit concerned about lettin' these girls out together. They can be a bit of a handful, and there are the rules the Squires gave me to follow…" Sarah wrung her hands.

"Not to worry, dear Sarah. I have plenty of experience with children. I have raised three, you know. All boys, granted, but handfuls just the same. We will be fine and dandy. It will do Ruth a world of good. Trust me."

Sarah sighed and ushered her guest into the parlor.

"Girls? There you are. Ready for a day in town? Are you going to introduce me to your friend, Ruth?"

"Hello, Mrs. Kirby, yes, this is Virginia Whitlow, my best friend. Ginny, meet Mrs. Kirby."

"Ginny…what a spunky name. It suits you. Where did you ever get that lovely dress? The green reminds me of the willow outside my window." She reached out to shake Ginny's hand.

"Mrs. Kirby, so nice to meet you. Thank you for the compliment. It's the newest fashion. Mother ordered it from the catalog. Isn't it divine?"

"Oh, do call me Elizabeth. I expect we will become fast friends, since Ruth will be part of our family."

Ginny giggled. "Okay, *Elizabeth.* That is exactly what I will do. Where are we going today?"

Elizabeth moved between the girls and encircled each waist. "Well, I think we will start with lunch at my favorite restaurant, Antoine's. It is the newest thing in town. Everybody is going there. Afterward, we can stop at all the good dress shops or any place either of you would like to go."

Both girls looked at one another. "Oh, Ginny, I have *so* wanted to go there. Mother thought it too extravagant."

"I know, Mother wouldn't take me, either. Are you sure it's all right? I didn't bring much money," Ginny said.

"I know people, dear. Put your money away. The treat is on me. I live with three boys remember? It is a blessed relief to spend a day with female companionship. Come on let's go."

The rain did not dampen the spirit of the day as they went from shop to shop, and lunch at Antoine's took Ruth's breath away. She reveled in its elegant décor, the well-dressed patrons, and the waiters' black tie uniforms. Even though she relished the sheer joy of dining in such a place, Ruth kept an eye on Mrs. Kirby. She wanted to like her, but her emotions remained mixed. *I need to catch her off guard, get her to admit she has ulterior motives. Why does she want me to marry her son – someone he doesn't know? It is not done any more.*

"We have so many parcels. I'll get my driver to stow them in the automobile. I would like to take afternoon tea at Rosie's. How does that sound, ladies? Afterward, we will take a walk in the park."

"In this rain, Mrs. Kirby? We'll get soaked," Ginny said.

"No we won't, Ginny, not with these." They stood by the mercantile store where a container full of umbrellas stood beside the door.

"Mr. Arnold, would you hold three of these for me? We are having tea at Rosie's, and we will be back for them."

"Why, of course, Mrs. Kirby." He pulled out three parasols and took them inside.

After an hour at Marilynne's Dress Emporium, Mrs. Kirby announced her need to rest and take refreshment. "Not as young as I use to be, ladies, and I'm certainly not use to a whole day of shopping. Plus, I want you to see Rosie's. It's down the block and to the right."

Arm in arm, the three women strolled the boardwalk until they reached their destination.

"Do you come here often?" Ruth admired the demitasse cups, the hanging plants, and colorful pots of geraniums. Multi-colored roses adorned every corner, and intricate lace curtains draped the windows. Music played in the background and gave the tearoom an elegant atmosphere.

"I try to come once a month, Ruth. It reminds me of home. It's a treat I indulge in...without my sons. They wouldn't appreciate the feminine setting." She laughed and swept a hand around the room.

After they devoured their teacakes, the women grew silent. The day was fast coming to a close.

"Ruth, I would like to know what you think of my son." Peter's mother lifted the teacup half way to her lips.

Startled, Ruth's cup clattered in the saucer. "Why, Mrs. Kirby, I do not really know him. How can I form an opinion?" Her heart sank. She did not want to talk about Peter Kirby, only enjoy this day with her best friend and this delightful woman. Deep down, she knew the subject would come up…and now that it had, the day became less enchanted.

"Oh, I know, Ruth, dear. You don't know him at all. Nevertheless, do you find him attractive? I mean that *is* an important attribute, don't you think? I know he finds you attractive."

"He does? He told you?" All of a sudden, her skin tingled, her heart raced.

Ginny giggled aloud. "Oh Ruthie, he likes you! This is so exciting."

"It is not, Ginny. Be quiet. I do *not* want to get married."

"Ruth, it's all right. I know it is a shock. Your mother and I have talked about this for weeks now. I want you to get to know Peter, not rush into anything. Lord knows, I want to see my son happy. These things happen all the time—marriages *are* arranged. For the most part, they turn out well. I can talk to your mother and father. Maybe we can push the wedding forward a month or two, give you and Peter time to get to know one another. You will like him, dear. He is a kind man, a gentle man, like his father. He provides for his two brothers and me and quit college to start his own business. You cannot find a more settled man. He takes responsibility to family seriously. You will be well cared for, Ruth."

"Exactly the problem, Mrs. Kirby. I do not want to be well cared for, I want to care for myself, see the world, travel, see new places, and do new things. I will not make a good wife to your son. I have already told him. You cannot force me." She rose from the table as if to leave, her face hot.

Elizabeth laid a hand on Ruth's arm. "Please, I'm sorry. We will talk of it no more, if you so wish. Are you ready for a walk around the park? Let's end the day on a pleasant note."

They left the tearoom, stopped for the umbrellas, and turned their attention to the plaza.

Ruth, surprised at Mrs. Kirby's silence, found curiosity got the better of her and, despite her resolve, wanted to know more. "You meant what you said? No more talk about Peter?"

Mrs. Kirby put her arm around Ruth's waist. "If that is your desire, dear. I like you and want to be friends whether you marry Peter or not. I would like an opportunity to change your mind about marriage, however."

"We can walk and we can talk, Mrs. Kirby, but it will not change my mind. I appreciate the day, and I hope I have found a new friend. But I still do not want to marry."

"I can understand your feelings, my dear. Marriage is hard, and you are so young. I once had those very thoughts myself. I changed my mind after I met my husband. We were married two months later. I never regretted a moment of it." The older woman's voice faltered.

Ginny jumped out in front of the others and gaped at Mrs. Kirby. "Your marriage was arranged? How old were you? I simply cannot imagine being told who to marry." Ginny exclaimed.

"Yes, my marriage was arranged. I was 17, like you and Ruth. Oh, I was afraid, angry, argued with my parents. However, once I met him, well…everything changed. He was so gallant and good-looking. I was swept off my feet. I never looked back, not once. Have you ever had a real boyfriend, Ruth? I had not. My husband was my very first encounter with the male of the species."

Ruth felt the heat rise to her cheeks. "No." Her heart jumped, her hands became clammy, and she had a funny tingle in her lower belly. It made her uncomfortable; she did not understand these feelings. *I hope she didn't see me blush. Had she really experienced the same reactions, or is she trying to make her son irresistible to me?*

The three women continued to promenade quietly along the lakeside. "You have those feelings, don't you, dear? I know you do. I saw your face when I mentioned a boyfriend. It's completely natural, what women *should* feel, although we are not to talk about it. In light of the fact your mother is not here, I feel I can approach the subject, since it is *my* son you will marry. You are practically part of the family. My son is handsome, don't you think? It would be different if your parents chose someone not so attractive. Do you want a home of your own, come and go as you please, decorate it yourself? Have your friends over—be part of society? A married woman giving dinner parties to the most influential people in town. Think of it, Ruth. It will be more freedom than you imagine. You can still travel. Get an education; make a difference in the world, all with a handsome husband on your arm encouraging you. You would eliminate the struggle and get to those dreams sooner. I only ask you think about it, Ruth. I will see what I can do with your parents to postpone the wedding a bit. You are young and vital, a force to be reckoned with, and your parents know it. They want to protect you, help you avoid the mistakes young women of this time make in their enthusiasm. Will you think about it?"

The rain came down a bit harder, making little pebble noises on their parasols. The lake was awash with white caps, and the wind picked up speed.

Ginny moved a bit closer to Mrs. Kirby. "Elizabeth, can you talk to *my* parents? It all sounds so perfect…the world handed to you on a platter. It is really a bit of instant independence. You should listen to her, Ruthie."

Ruth shot her friend a dirty look.

Elizabeth addressed Ruth's friend. "Ginny, you know I cannot talk to your parents. I don't know them. The Squires and I have known each other for a while now. It is an idea developed slowly, over time, not a spur of the moment decision. Things will happen for you in good time, Ginny, and think of it; you can visit and be a part of Ruth's new life."

Ginny laughed. "I know, I was teasing. I am glad we met you. I hope we will be fast friends. What about you, Ruth? You are so quiet."

"Yes, Ruth, you have not said anything. Are you open to my idea? Can we give it some time?" Elizabeth asked.

Ruth kept her head down, watching the ground as they walked. The rain made little puddles, and she watched in fascination as her shoes disturbed them. She thought of her life like those puddles. One day, life was normal, undisturbed, and the next, distorted and unclear.

"Are you listening? What are you going to do?" Ginny implored.

Ruth looked at her best friend, then at Mrs. Kirby. She liked this woman. She was friendly and talked to her like an adult instead of a child, and her voice was soft and kind. Her thoughts turned to Peter. Yes, he is handsome and makes a good living. Questions whirled in her mind while she tried to sort out what Peter's mother offered—freedom. She longed for it. The proposal sounded good, but would she really have freedom? Would he turn into one of those men who expected his wife to be servant to his needs? She was not prepared to make such a decision. "Mrs. Kirby. You have been so kind. This was a most pleasant day, a great diversion, and I like you. You are a lovely person. Your son is very handsome, I admit. I would like to take you up on your offer to postpone any decision right now. Could you talk to Mother, get her to agree? I promise I will think about all you said today."

Mrs. Kirby placed her arm around both girls' waists. "Of course I will, dear. Don't you worry, we will figure this out. I would like for you and Ginny to come to dinner tomorrow night. It will give you a chance to meet my other boys and talk to Peter a little more. What do you say?"

Panic turned her skin clammy. "I don't know. I'm not sure I am ready. I need to breathe a little, get use to the idea. No, I don't think I should." She wriggled free of the older woman's embrace.

Ginny grasped Ruth's hand and forced her to look into her eyes. "Ruthie, think about this. If you are not willing to work on this, your mother is more likely to force you to marry quickly. Make her think you are considering the idea, otherwise, she will think you are stalling. I know your mother as well as you. She won't like it if you aren't co-operating. Think about it. We have spent many years figuring ways to thwart her. This is one of those times. Give her what she wants until you figure out how to get around her. Remember?"

"You have a point, I guess. She probably *would* push me harder if I resisted." Ruth's heart rate slowed a bit, she sucked in a deep breath, and let it out slowly. "What time should we be there? Will you send a car for us?"

"Of course. This is a wise choice, my dear. I am confident we will all get along famously. I look forward to dinner. Is there anything you prefer, any special dish? I am a very good cook, although, I do have a girl who helps with the meals. Not as young as I use to be, you know," Mrs. Kirby chattered.

"Anything you fix will be fine. I'm not a picky eater. It is very kind of you, really."

"What time, Elizabeth? I have to tell *my* mother." Ginny asked.

"Let's say six o'clock. Is that good for you?"

The walk back to the car was pleasant. The conversation turned to their shopping escapade, their purchases, and the fancy lunch they shared.

In the back of Ruth's mind, a plan formed. *I will go along for now, but mother's secret letters will be my way out. I only have to decide when to use them.*

Chapter Six

Peter watched his mother motor off in the used Ford Model T to pick up his future wife for a day of shopping. The sky was gray, matching his mood, and a light drizzle continued to fall. Did he really want to marry a girl he barely knew? It was clear she had no interest in marriage. Why was Mother so cheerful about this? Ruth did have the most amazing eyes though—and her skin, like milk. She *was* beautiful. He sighed, loaded up the last of his bottles, and hopped aboard his French Baur milk wagon. He was proud of his wagon and horses, bought with the money he had saved for college. His own business kept body and soul together right now.

During his route, there was plenty of time to think about his future. He worked from dawn to dusk most days. This was a slow route today and enabled him to get a later start to accommodate for Mother's rendezvous. Patch and Bunny clopped along at the regular pace, and the rhythm lulled him into euphoria. He did his best thinking during this time. A man of purpose, he needed to see the sense in this arranged union before he could commit to it. Mother met the Squires in church and began comparing notes on the single fate of both their offspring. Before Ruth's errant behavior, he knew they had conspired to get him and Ruth together.

"Good morning, Peter!"

The singsong voice of his first stop, Mrs. Jones, shook him out of his reverie. "Good morning, ma'am. A little bit of a wet day today." He swung off the truck and hoisted her order down. The bottles clanged on the way to the porch. He noticed Mrs. Jones stood rooted to the spot, as she did every morning, and watched him approach. She also remained there when he returned to the truck. Out of the corner of his eye, he noticed she tracked his every move. He really didn't understand why women did that. It is only milk. Surely, these women had other things to do. The attention made him uncomfortable sometimes. It was the same at the next house, and the next.

One lady asked him how he maintained his strong arms and kept his waist so trim. "The loadin' and unloadin' I guess, ma'am." He turned quickly to hide the blush he felt rush to his face.

He hurried to finish the route and get back to the house, although, trepidation attached itself to his mood. What if Ruth told Mother there was no way she would marry him. He had to admit, she danced in his thoughts all day. Her chocolate eyes, and the curve of her figure beneath the green dress, aroused him. "I haven't had these thoughts since I was a boy of 15. What has become of me?" The horses whinnied at the sound of his voice, no help at all.

◆◆◆◆

The house stood quiet when Ruth entered the foyer. Ginny wanted to stay and engage in girl talk, but she sent her away, in no mood to listen to her prattle.

"Sarah?" She called the name softly. Silence the only response. The loud creak of the stairs echoed in the large house. The doorway of her room was open, but she swept passed it and continued down the hall. This was Sarah's usual shopping day and the perfect time to examine the letters in Mother's closet. The air was chilly, but sweat dampened her palms. She decided to go through the guest room. Her heart raced when the doorknob offered no resistance. She flung the door open. The bed was made. There was no clutter on the dressing table, no sign of anyone.

"Are ya at it again, Ruthie?"

She whirled to face the voice. "Damn! You scared the life out of me, Sarah. Don't sneak up on someone like that. I wasn't doing anything, only making sure you have done your job properly."

"I have done my job proper, to be sure, young lady, and you watch what is comin' out of yer mouth. I suggest you get back to your room. Or, would ya be wantin' me to tell your mother about your little escapade in her room? You've had a full day. I want to hear all about it, but right now, I must get your supper and make sure all is put aright. A wire came from your folks. They will be arrivin' home day after tomorrow. Better prepare."

The hall felt hollow, unfamiliar. She watched Sarah hurry down the stairs. After her day with Mrs. Kirby, the evening stretched long and lonely. Her parents would be home soon and plans made. Was it supposed to be this way? She felt transparent, invisible, as if the only thing that mattered was the *proper* thing. Never mind her feelings, or desires.

Leaden feet moved toward her bedroom door. Was it all a dream? Would she wake up and find it had all been a horrible nightmare? The door remained open as she sat upon the bed in her room. The hallway summoned her, and thoughts of the perfumed letters beckoned.

◆◆◆◆

Elizabeth's arrival at the cottage caused the familiar chaos of two pre-teen boys scrambling for attention from the wandering family members. Peter happened to drive up immediately behind her. "Mother, Peter. Did you see her? What is she like? Was she pretty? Are you married yet? When do *we* get to meet her? What did you buy us?" Both blond-headed boys chattered over the other, vying for center stage.

Elizabeth laughed, and she and Peter each grabbed a boy around the shoulders and pulled them into the house. "You will see soon enough, Charlie. She is coming for dinner tomorrow night. Now go finish the chores assigned this morning. I know you haven't completed your tasks. You probably peered out of the window the whole time, waiting for us to get home. And you, Joseph, you have not finished the list I gave *you* this morning, I'll bet." Elizabeth ruffled the hair of her youngest.

They scampered off, and Elizabeth turned to her oldest son. "All is well, Peter. I believe I have won her over, just as I said. She agreed to come to dinner tomorrow."

"I'm not so confident, Mother. She is not quite a woman yet. Her mind will shift back and forth. Maybe when she sees Charlie and Joseph, she will fall in love with the family as well as me. I think she really likes you."

"She is a delightful girl, and yes, we connected. It will work out all right, my dear. It truly will."

"I should go to the bank tomorrow, Mother. There is business to attend. The prospect of a new wife changes the face of things."

"And I must ready things for our dinner with Ruth tomorrow. I will have a full day, I expect."

Chapter Seven

The sun waxed brighter today than the day before, and Eric Horton whistled a jaunty tune, a spring in his step on the way to the office. Tomorrow the Squires will arrive home, and he would present his plan to the clueless couple. "They get what *they* want, and I get what *I* want." He could virtually see his new promotion, and the status it would afford him. Decorators needed to be hired, gardeners consulted. The house he had his eye on was fresh in his mind. It was a gorgeous Effington structure, exquisite design—perfectly maintained, but needed a woman's touch. Ruth was young, a breath of fresh air. He would feel young and vital again, a second chance at youth.

The bank bustled around the new business of the day, the noise rhythmic and soothing. When silence settled over the main lobby, he looked up to see a striking, blond gentleman enter and walk to the nearest teller. He leaned over and whispered something to the young woman. She nodded in Eric's direction. The man swung around and walked with a determined step toward him.

"May I help you, sir?" Eric rose and reached out a hand.

"Yes, my name is Peter Kirby, and I need to adjust my accounts in order to accommodate an addition to our family."

"Congratulations, a new baby! Please, have a seat. Is your wife doing well, Mr. Kirby? Is it a boy or a girl?"

"Ah, no, no. It is not a baby. I don't have a wife, yet. That is why I am here. I need to set up a household account for my betrothed. We will marry in a month, and I want her to have access to an account to run the house."

"Oh, I see. Yes, yes, of course, a new wife. I can appreciate your need to get things off on the right foot. I, too, am to be newly married. So, of course, I can guide you with this matter very easily."

"Ah, we have something in common. Best wishes to you, as well." Peter uncrossed his legs. "I am in a bit of a hurry. If you could…"

"Certainly." Eric pulled the necessary forms from his desk drawer and placed them on the table. "Now, what is your bride's full name?"

"No, you don't understand. I run a milk route, and I am late. Can you give me the forms I need so I can take them with me? We can fill them out and bring them back. Is that acceptable?"

"Of course, Mr. Kirby, I understand completely. Let me put these in a folder for you. Bring them back at your convenience."

The two men stood and shook hands.

"Before you go, Mr. Kirby, may I ask your wife's first name?"

Peter threw her name over his shoulder as he took long strides toward the door. "Ruth."

◆◆◆◆

Elizabeth leaned over the pot of homemade beef soup to savor the aroma of the tried and true family recipe. She chose it with Ruth in mind. Her secret ingredient would, without a doubt, peak her future daughter-in-law's interest. "Once Ruth asks about the unknown addition, I will know she is hooked." She checked on the roast in the oven and smiled. *Coming along nicely.*

One by one, she checked off the items needed for the remainder of the meal. "Wheat rolls, Golden Glow Salad, fluffy mashed potatoes, steamed marmalade, and my special Chocolate Chiffon Pie. That should do the trick. She will see we eat very well. Now, I need to make sure the table is ready."

She was bent over the buffet in the dining room counting linen napkins, when a shadow snuffed the sunlight from the room.

"What, who? Oh, Peter, you startled me. What are you doing home this time of day?"

"I didn't mean to frighten you, Mother. I merely want to drop these papers off before I lose them. I went to the bank this morning, and Mr. Horton assembled the papers to set up a household account for Ruth. I told him I would return them once everything was settled." Peter's long stride carried him across the room quickly. "What is that wonderful smell? Did you get carried away? We don't want her to think we are wealthy, you know. It's been a while since I've noticed such rich aromas in the house." He pecked her on the cheek and surveyed the abundant dining table, Mother's finest china, and the sparkling silver and water goblets of German crystal.

She returned the kiss. "I don't want her to think we are simpletons, either. She is used to a certain standard of living. I only wish to reaffirm her life style won't change much, dear."

Peter smiled broadly, and his eyes twinkled. "She will think we set table like this every week night.

Surely you don't intend for Charlie and Joseph to eat on the good china."

"They can behave when properly coerced, Peter. I have promised them plum pudding if they will act like perfect gentleman."

The two laughed together, and Peter took his leave and returned to work.

Pleased to see her son in a happier mood, she hummed and resumed the preparations. She knew he found Ruth attractive, but his kind nature sympathized with the girl's situation. *I will make this work. Only an hour before school is out. I have enough time to finish dinner and make myself presentable. This cozy house and warm reception will win her over.*

◆◆◆◆

Eric Horton stood in the doorway of his office, mouth agape. Surely, he heard him wrong. *Did he say Ruth?*

"Anything amiss, Mr. Horton?" The head teller stopped in front of his desk.

"No, no, nothing, Mrs. Dudley. The young man…I wonder if I've seen him somewhere before. He looks very familiar." Her gray hair, swept too tightly into a severe bun, and overly tight navy business suit did nothing to soften the sour look on the secretary's face. Eric found her a very unpleasant woman most of the time. He sat down in his chair and opened a drawer, in a gesture of dismissal.

"Well, our work wouldn't get finished if we contemplated every customer who came through the door, would it Mr. Horton?"

"Of course not, Mrs. Dudley, I don't make a habit of assessing our customers. This one caught my eye. Now if you'll excuse me, I do have work to do."

She gave him a curt nod and went back to her station.

"Why am I to suffer the displeasure of these old biddies? When I am promoted, I will see to it they all get an early retirement." He bent to his work, but his thoughts went back to Peter. "Ruth is a common name, purely coincidental. I'll make a point to call his attention to this fact. He'll get a jolly laugh out of it, I'm sure." He looked around the bank, satisfied. Soon, he will control it all, and life would change forever.

The office chair squeaked when he leaned back to study the ceiling. *The Squires come home tomorrow. I must make an appointment for them to come to the bank. Yes, it is much better if they come here…more formal and professional. It will make a bigger impact on them within the confines of the bank. They should not bring Ruth, however. She cannot be aware of the circumstances, only be convinced this is a perfect match for her. Being the wife of the Vice President of the bank should appeal to her, the thought of a fancy new house – why any girl would jump at the chance. Tomorrow can't come too soon.*

Chapter Eight

"HOW do I look, Ruthie? Do I look like a woman of the world, a matron of sophistication?" Ginny whirled around in her newly purchased dress.

"You look fine, Ginny, stop preening. One might think you are the one to marry," Ruth replied.

"Oh gosh, I wish it *were* me. He is so handsome. I can't believe you are not completely head over heels," Ginny exclaimed.

"Oh hush. Here's the car for us. Will you please act as if you have *some* sense?"

"What's happened, Ruth? You use to be the first to slap aside propriety. Gone from girl to matron in one day? Come on; go along for the ride at least. You're not getting married *tonight*, after all."

Ruth rode in silence to Peter's house, nerves twisting knots in her stomach. *I will not eat a bite I am sure.* Maybe she had changed in just a day. Meeting Peter's mother calmed her a bit. *I wish Mother were more like Mrs. Kirby. Mother is so drab, so plain, it's hard for me to imagine her as a girl – ever.*

Thoughts of her mother brought to mind the drab dresses in the forbidden closet…and the ball gowns on the *other* side – and of course, the letters. *I must go back and get them.* She shook her head. *I absolutely cannot think of those bizarre events this evening.* On one hand, terror gripped her, on the other, curiosity. While she took to Mrs. Kirby right away, the thought of being maneuvered into marriage left a bad taste in her mouth. The setting of this evening would determine her acceptance of the relationship with Peter Kirby.

The car continued to move toward the outskirts of Detroit proper. "They must live in the country," she whispered to her friend. "I guess I hadn't thought about where he lived."

"Ooh, a country estate. How exciting," Ginny replied.

"I hardly think he owns an estate. He is a milkman, remember. I only hope it's not a run down old shack.

The car turned down a country lane and pulled in front of a cottage style dwelling. A white picket fence, a lovely tree-lined driveway, and empty, but well-groomed flowerbeds adorned the front of the house. Sturdy shrubs softened the stark winter landscape.

She began to relax. Although it was not the stately form of her house in the city, it had a warm, tranquil atmosphere. Fleecy, white snow softened the lack of color, dressed the trees branches, and blanketed the lawn like a down comforter.

Ginny pointed towards the house. "Look, it's such a lovely cottage. You could have horses out here, and dogs. Your mother would never let you have a pet in the city," she cried.

In a low voice she replied, "It *is beautiful.* Look at all the flowerbeds and trees. I can just imagine the beauty in the spring time."

The minute the car slowed to a stop, two boys bounded from the house. "It's her! It's Peter's new wife. Hello, Hello."

"Well, hello indeed," Ruth answered as she exited the automobile. "Now, which one of you is Charlie, and which one is Joseph?"

"I'm Charlie, *that* one is Joseph," answered the tallest boy.
"Pleased to meet you, Charlie. I'm Ruth."
"We know. We know. Peter told us all about you. You *are* as beautiful as he says," answered the youngest.
She knew a blush rushed to her cheeks. *So, he has told his brothers all about me… that I'm beautiful.*
"Who's this one?" asked Charlie. "Is she a wife for me?"
"Heavens, no, this is Ginny, my very best friend. She has come as a sort of chaperone, tonight. Ginny, this is Charlie, and this one over here is Joseph."
Ginny bent to shake hands when a call from the porch interrupted them.
"Boys, enough, it's not polite to bombard two young women like that. Let them get into the house."
The voice was Elizabeth's. She wiped her hands on a towel, and untied her white ruffle apron. Dressed in a beige coatdress, not too fancy, not too plain, she looked radiant. Her hair was up in a becoming French twist, and the glow on her face showed pure happiness at the prospect of her company.
The two boys took a hand of each of the girls and pulled them toward the front door. Laughing, they all stumbled into the house, out of breath.
"Now boys, you know the tasks I have set out for you once our guests arrived. I suggest you get to them." One hand on her hip, she patted the bottom of the smallest boy, and they scurried off to do her bidding. "I am sorry, ladies. Those two keep me hopping, as you can see. They are so excited to meet you. I did not tell them about Ginny coming for fear

they couldn't contain themselves. Please won't you sit here in the parlor?"

"Where's Peter, Mrs. Kirby?" Ginny asked.

"He will be along, dear. He started late on his route this morning. He had some business in town," she turned and smiled broadly at Ruth.

"Is there anything we can do to help? We are not use to being waited on, you know. We usually eat in the kitchen when our parents have guests," Ruth stated.

"It's time you had experience with a real dinner party then. We are not as regal as the city folks, but we certainly know how to put together a *proper* dinner party. You and Ginny rest, and I will see to the soup. Peter should be along any moment. I hope you are hungry. I've made his favorite tonight."

"It smells wonderful. I didn't realize I was hungry until I walked in the door. The aroma is simply mouth-watering." Ginny flounced down on the sofa.

The girls fell silent and surveyed the parlor filled with hundreds of porcelain and ceramic figurines. Fidgety, Ruth walked across the room to inspect a set of fragile ballerinas. She reached out her hand, but quickly pulled it back.

"Good move, Ruth. Wouldn't you hate to break something on your first visit?" Ginny moved behind her and peered over her shoulder.

Ruth reached out again. "They are so delicate, so precise. Every detail is etched on each figure."

"It was my father's specialty—how he made a living. Mother could not bear to part with these after his passing. It was a very harrowing experience to pack each one and transport them. She never could have survived if one had broken on the trip."

Ruth turned abruptly, bumping into Ginny. "Oh, Peter, you startled us. I didn't hear you come in. We were admiring these beautiful pieces. Your father created them? He must have been talented indeed."

"He was an extraordinary man, yes," Peter replied.

Elizabeth appeared in the doorway. "Ah, I see you are home, son. Dinner is close to ready. Could you round up Charlie and Joseph? Make sure they wash their hands."

"Certainly, Mother. Ladies, will you please excuse me for a moment?" He stopped to peck his mother on the cheek.

Ruth's eyes lingered on Peter's back, his broad shoulders and the cut of his trousers sent unfamiliar shivers through her nether regions.

Ginny poked her in the ribs, made her jump, and whispered, "Put your eyes back in their sockets, Ruth. You're too obvious."

Ruth, cheeks aflame, darted a look at Mrs. Kirby, who smiled like a Cheshire cat and turned back toward the kitchen.

The two young women returned to their seats and continued to peruse the room.

"Ginny, she must have a maid to clean and dust all these treasures, although, I would be surprised if she trusted anyone else with the task. I bet it takes the better part of the day to finish it."

Ginny faced her friend square on. "Don't try to weasel out of this one. I saw the way you looked at Peter. You showed true desire watching him walk away. You can't lie to your best friend, Ruth."

"Stop it, Ginny. This isn't the time or place to discuss this. I noticed how tall he was, that's all. I didn't remember him being that tall, now drop it. We still have to get through dinner."

"What ever you say, liar." Ginny giggled and settled back in her chosen overstuffed chair.

Before long, Peter returned and offered each girl an arm. "Ready, ladies? Let me escort you to the table."

When they entered the dining area, the two younger boys already sat in their places. They looked as if they were very use to this kind of occasion, hands folded in their laps, hair brushed to a shine. Pink cheeks announced a recent scrubbing.

Elizabeth motioned for Peter to take the head of the table and placed Ruth to his right. She took her spot on his left and Ginny to the left of her. All the women stood while Peter made the rounds to seat each one.

Ruth watched Peter and his mother join hands, and Charlie and Joseph did the same. Elizabeth reached for Ginny's hand. When Peter laid his hand on Ruth's, she became dizzy from the shock of it. He bowed his head and began the blessing. His deep resonant voice captured her, mesmerized her as he said the prayer. She forgot to bow her head and close her eyes, but continued to gaze at him completely enraptured.

"Dear Lord, we are thankful today to have such lovely guests to add to our table and pray you will bless this food to each of us. May our visit be pleasant and restful. Please bless our dear mother who prepared this meal and please, Lord, keep Charlie and Joseph out of mischief this evening. In God's name we pray, Amen." He lifted his head and winked at his brothers.

Ruth felt lost when he relinquished her hand. A quick glance at Elizabeth confirmed she had watched her through the entire blessing.

"Mrs. Kirby, the soup smells divine. I can hardly wait to try it," Ginny babbled on about how her stomach rumbled.

Meanwhile, Ruth's appetite left her, altogether.

Peter served each person and ladled the soup as if he performed this task every day. Not one drop spilled.

She picked up the soupspoon and prepared to taste her first sample, awkwardness suddenly rearing its ugly head. Lucky for her, Mother taught her the proper use of utensils and their place at table.

The two boys finished their respective bowls, and with a clatter of spoons, demanded more.

While Peter's mother admonished them about their manners, Ruth tasted the soup. Her head jerked up, surprised at the pleasant warmth on her palate. "Why, Mrs. Kirby, this is most tasty. It is unusual though. What's your secret?"

"It's an old family recipe brought from Holland, a secret spice mixed with other spices, and blend myself. I have a garden out back in which I grow each one, dry, and store them, so I'll always have them on hand. Only family members will be privy to all the information, though." She winked at Ruth and returned to her own fare.

Ruth determined not to say another word. Peter sat silent.

The next course introduced the roast beef, and again, Ruth realized she'd never quite tasted anything like it before. It was tangy and full-bodied. "I suppose you have a special ingredient for the pot roast you can't share with us also, Mrs. Kirby? I don't believe I have ever had pot roast with quite this kind of zing."

"Mother is an artful and skilled cook, Ruth. We are often surprised by her secrets and experiments. I hope it's all to your liking."

"Oh, it is, Peter. It's all lovely. I wasn't really hungry when I arrived, but the aromas set my juices flowing." She immediately wished she could take back the last comment. Heat rose to her face, and she looked down at the plate, embarrassed.

There was polite conversation as the meal progressed, and finally, Elizabeth brought in the chocolate chiffon pie.

"I really couldn't, Mrs. Kirby. I'm completely stuffed," Ruth said.

Mrs. Kirby placed the pie in the middle of the table. "Why don't you and Peter take a walk? The night air might help to stimulate your hunger once more. It would disappoint me if you didn't taste my special pie. It's Peter's favorite. Ginny, maybe you would like to help me and the boys straighten up this mess?"

The two boys whined in unison. "Oh, Mother, must we? Why does Peter never have to help in the kitchen?"

"Charlie and Joseph, do as Mother asks. This is no way to behave in front of company," Peter said, his look stern.

"Wait, I would love to help Mrs. Kirby in the kitchen. Let the boys off the hook tonight. I'd love the time to visit with my new friend." Ginny laid a hand on Peter's arm and looked at the two boys.

Hopeful eyes returned to Peter, and the boys moved between him and their newfound hero.

"Well, I don't know. It is part of their tasks in the evening to help with the dishes," he answered.
"But this is a special night, lots of extra work. I'll take their place and give them a night off."
Elizabeth nodded to Peter, and he relented, at which time, the boys grabbed Ginny around the waist and cried 'thank you' into her skirt.
Everyone laughed, and the boys scampered away. Peter offered his arm to Ruth. "Would you like to wander through the garden? It's a bit chilly, and there's nothing growing right now, but Mother keeps it neat and clean, even in winter. Maybe we could get to know each other better. I promise I won't bite."
She laid her hand on Peter's arm and smiled. "Yes, it sounds lovely. Maybe I can spot your mother's secret ingredient while we're out there."
Peter laughed. He reached for his mother's shawl and took his time placing it around her shoulders.
They left the front porch, and he guided her around the back of the cottage where the real garden stretched out in front of her. She reveled in the well cared for walkways winding through the bushes and shrubs. At the end of each turn sat a concrete bench, and Peter asked if she'd like to sit when they came upon one.
She waited until they arrived at the back of the garden before she acquiesced. "I don't believe I've seen the spice garden yet, Peter. Is it hidden?" They sat on the bench, and she felt the warmth of his body next to hers, inviting, yet uncomfortable at the same time.
"Ruth, I don't want to talk of spices or gardens tonight. There will be time enough for that later. I

want to talk about us…you and me. Your parents arrive home tomorrow with all their plans made. I wanted to tell you I have dreamed about you. I cannot get you out of my mind. I need to know if you feel the same way. Do you desire me, or think I am a big oaf, unacceptable for marriage? Does my family live too simple for your taste? These are all things I must know before we take this step of marriage."

His hand lay atop hers. The heat of his touch consumed her focus, and she struggled to hear his words. She lowered her gaze and looked at the muscled hand clasped around hers.

"Peter, I don't…I just…please. I don't know what I feel at the moment. I am only seventeen. I've had no experience in the matters of love. I haven't had a proper boyfriend yet. Yes, I have feelings, small flutters of excitement. Heat settles in my body in unmentionable places. It's all so confusing. Is it love or simply desire? You will have to help me sort this all out. You have much more experience at this sort of thing than I."

Peter removed his hand from hers and stood up. "Of course, forgive me. You are but a girl. Although, if you think I have experience with women, you are sadly mistaken. My father died as I was going out into the world. He had been a hard taskmaster and insisted I concentrate on my studies. There was little time to think about women. After his death, I became the head of the household, and every waking moment is spent on how to secure this family's future. Maybe we are both naïve when it comes to matters of the heart, but we have no time to figure it out. Our parents will push us to make a decision."

He sat beside her again and turned her toward him. "You said you felt desire, heat, and flutters. That's a start. You must have an attraction to me. I'm not utterly repulsive to you. Maybe it's enough. Maybe it is all my mother and father had. They built their love on just that. Shall we try, Ruth?"

She looked into his eyes. "I suppose we can try, Peter, although, I must warn you, I'm very headstrong. I have a bad temper, I'm an only child used to having the focus on me. You are such a loving family, I'm not sure I'll fit."

"You're a breath of fresh air. Mother never had a daughter. She will love having you around, and the boys adore you already. You'll fit in fine."

They were silent for while. Peter removed his hands from her shoulders and covered her folded hands. After a moment, he raised a hand and lifted her head to meet his eyes. "May I kiss you, Ruth?"

Panic engulfed her, and she wanted to run. She turned away and felt him stiffen at the rejection.

"I don't think I'm ready. It's not that I don't want to, but I have never kissed a boy before."

Peter relaxed a little and touched her face, softly. "I'll not rush you, I promise. With your parents' return tomorrow, I am afraid we will have little time for privacy to actually find out about each other. This might very well be one of the few times we have alone before our wedding night. Do you understand what I mean, Ruth?"

Her face warmed at his implication. The wedding night loomed ahead of her … it was unfathomable. She stood up and broke the spell cast over them.

Instead of dropping the subject, Peter encircled her with his arms and kissed her full on the mouth. She stiffened, but he did not relent. His lips were hot, but soft and yearning. Shock rippled through her as his tongue began to flit around at the opening of her mouth. Just as she was ready to yield, to allow him in, he pulled away.

He hung his head. "I am so sorry, Ruth. I couldn't help myself. I have wanted to taste those ruby lips all day. While on my route, I could think of nothing else. Please forgive me. I'm ashamed, and I wouldn't blame you if you ran like the wind and had nothing more to do with me." He turned away.

"Wait." Ruth didn't recognize her own voice. "Peter, wait." She touched his arm.

He turned back to her. "Yes?" he replied.

She couldn't meet his gaze. "It wasn't altogether unpleasant. I mean, it was rather nice. I wonder if we might try it once more."

"You mean it? You liked it? How wonderful, because I thought it was amazing. Oh Ruth, maybe, just maybe this will work for us." His eyes sparkled like sapphires in the crisp night air. He reached out gently for her, and this time, she dared to put her arms around him. To reach him, she stood on tiptoes, and the closeness of his body excited her. He pressed against her lithe frame, and she fought the desire to melt into him. His lips touched hers, lightly at first, and then more demanding. It lasted an eternity, and she forgot, a few feet away, sat his mother and her best friend.

They parted, and neither spoke, only gazed into each other's eyes.

"You feel it too, don't you?" Peter whispered.

"I'm not sure what it is I feel. I only know I want to feel it again."

"I think we should go inside before Mother becomes suspicious. It wouldn't do to look undisciplined in the eyes of her or your best friend." He reached down and pecked her on the cheek.

"Wait, what's that? There in the bushes…someone giggled."

Peter moved toward the sound, reached into the bush, and drew out his younger brother by the ear. "Charlie, does Mother know you're out here spying on us? Where is your brother, Joseph? The two of you are inseparable, so I know he's close by," Peter admonished.

"Here he is, over here, behind this shrub." Ruth parted the branches and out stepped the younger Kirby.

"What are we to do with you? Are you going to run and tell Mother what you saw?" Peter asked. "I will thrash you myself if you breathe one word. Now, off with you both." He smiled. "Well, it looks like we've been caught. Nothing to do now but to marry, I suppose. I wouldn't want to soil your reputation."

"I…I do not know what to say. Do you suppose they will tell?" she gasped.

"I'm teasing you, Ruth. Those two are too afraid of my wrath to say one word to Mother."

"So, you have a temper? Do you get very angry?" All of a sudden, the heat she experienced, only moments ago, turned cold, and the doubt and anxiety returned.

"I'm the only male authority they know. They were very young when father died. No, I don't have a terrible temper. I am firm, and they know what I say is what I mean. I have tried to treat them as Father did me. He was my only example. Please don't worry, that is not my nature. Now, I think we need to get back to the house before Mother *does* get suspicious."

They walked, hand in hand, through the sleeping garden—back to reality, the two younger boys nowhere in sight.

The kitchen was finished, and Ruth was well aware of the smiles on both Mrs. Kirby's and Ginny's faces. Did they know? Had the boys told them what they saw?

As they prepared to leave, she felt compelled to give Mrs. Kirby a small hug. "Thank you so much for dinner. It was delicious, very special, and the chiffon pie was excellent. I'm glad I found room for it after all. Tell the two boys good night for me. You made it very easy to get to know all of you. I suppose we will see each other very soon. Mother and Father will be home tomorrow."

Elizabeth returned the hug. "You and Ginny are welcome here any time. I hope our next meeting is a pleasant one between all of us...you, *and* your parents."

Peter cleared his throat. "Mother, do you suppose it would be improper of me to escort Ruth home, alone in my milk wagon? Ginny, would you mind going home by car? I'd like to speak to Ruth alone before we meet with her parents."

"I think it'll be perfectly fine, dear."

"It's okay with me, too, Peter. Your driver is very kind. It'll be an adventure for me, out in the evening, alone with my own driver. How grown up am I?" Ginny replied.

Hand in hand, they saw Ginny safely to the car. Ruth took notice of Peter's mother in the window as she watched them approach the milk wagon and saw the look of satisfaction on her face.

Peter circled his hands around her waist and lifted her like a feather to the driver's seat. She didn't protest.

"Do you like horses, Ruth?" Bunny neighed when she heard Peter's voice.

"Yes, very much, I seldom get a chance to ride though."

"That's wonderful. Then, you're not afraid." He took a deep breath. "It's a clear night for a change, a good night for a leisurely ride home. We can talk."

The steady rhythm of the horse's hooves on the cobblestone and the gentle sway of the wagon soothed her. She reflected on the kisses they shared in the garden. The schoolgirl escape from her window, a few nights ago, faded. In the blink of an eye, she was engaged, experienced her first kiss, and felt the heat of passion. *Am I falling in love? How can all this happen in only a few days?*

Peter broke the silence. "You're very quiet. Having second thoughts?"

She tilted her head toward him. "Do you really want to know?" Her mood mischievous, she wanted to tease him, to flirt a little, a glimpse of her old self.

He looked down and smiled. "Yes, I would like to know. I have to admit I'm insecure when it comes to your thoughts. You could have a change of heart, and I would be none the wiser. I want to get to know the real you." The horses slowed, and he flicked the rein softly. Their heads bobbed and picked up the pace once more.

In a bold move, she took his hand. "I was thinking of the kisses in the garden, Peter. I liked the sensation, and I liked the blood rushing in my veins. I want to feel it again. Are you shocked?"

"Shocked no…excited, yes. I thought you might feel compromised. I have great respect for you. Look, there's a small clearing. May I stop for a moment?"

She nodded her approval. "I'd be disappointed if you didn't."

The horses followed his direction and came to a stop under a willow tree. Peter set the brake and turned toward her. "You're beautiful in the moonlight. Your black eyes sparkle, your milk white skin glows. I want to kiss you again."

She turned her face toward the town to hide the blush she knew must be there. "Peter, look at the lights of the city. This is such a beautiful setting, like in a story."

"Do you want me to kiss you or not."

"Yes, please, kiss me." Their lips met, and this time, Ruth parted her lips as he slipped his tongue between them. He explored the deep recesses of her sweet mouth, and her breathing stopped. He pressed, more forceful, and she felt his need. It matched hers. She had never felt like this. It surprised her that a woman *could* feel this way.

The male anatomy was a mystery to her. She and Ginny would giggle about bulging muscles, dreamy eyes; the fine cut of a suit on a man. Now, her curiosity was piqued, and wanted to know more. She yielded to him, melted into him. It felt like she was being devoured.

With a rough abruptness, Peter pulled her away from him. "Not now, Ruth, not like this. We must control ourselves. It must be right when it happens. I'm at the brink of not being able to stop myself, and I must not put you in that position."

She whimpered slightly. "I don't care, Peter. I want to know you ... know what it's like. My blood's hot, and it won't cool down."

A slight breeze blew and lifted her hair. He brushed a strand away from her face. "You will, my darling, you will on our wedding night. This is what I hoped would happen, that we would feel this way toward one another. Right now, I need to get you home. We have a big day ahead of us...your parents and all. Sarah must be beside herself with worry."

She turned away from Peter. "I don't care about Sarah, and I certainly don't care about my parents. I've found you, and I don't want to let you go."

He grabbed her shoulders and forced her to look at him again. "Ruth, please do not act a child. You must convince your parents you are grown up enough for marriage. You must get a hold of yourself and do your duty. They must not see we desire one another, or they will keep us apart until the wedding. Don't you see? We have to play the game so we might continue to steal moments together before we're wed."

Her shoulders slumped, and she bowed her head. "I'm sorry Peter. I am still a child I suppose. You stirred something in me; something I didn't know was there. It will be hard to control, but I'm not sure I could bear not seeing you for a whole month, and to think, we only met three days ago. It's so hard to believe."

With his index finger, he raised her chin. "That's my girl. Our parents think they have control right now, and we must do their bidding. Let's take control of our own destiny, my sweetness. Let's play the game with them."

"Yes, Peter, yes. We can work together so we might find opportunity to see one another. It suits my rebellious nature to pull one over on my parents. I like your idea, Peter. I promise to behave like a woman you'll be proud to have on your arm."

With their heads together, Peter urged Patch and Bunny forward. As they entered the road once more, he bent to kiss her, softly. A sweet kiss, one she didn't need to return. They didn't speak for the rest of the ride home; there was no need, for there was perfect harmony between them. Love changed everything. Ruth would get her freedom from her parents *and* a man who stirred her blood, and heightened her sense of adventure. She was secretly thankful she chose to escape from her bedroom window.

Chapter Nine

The commotion downstairs woke her, and for a moment, couldn't remember the surroundings. The dream placed her in a grassy, clearing, bodice torn, and lips bruised with the desire of Peter Kirby. Her breath came in gasps as consciousness returned.

"Ruth, Ruth, wake up. Are you ill? Why are you moaning? You feel hot, fevered. I knew I shouldn't have let you out in the night air last night. Mr. Kirby was out of line. He should have sent you home in the auto with Ginny instead of riding atop the milk wagon like a common girl. You probably cost me my job, Ruth. Now wake up." Sarah shook her, hard.

"Wait, Sarah, wait. I'm not ill…a dream, that's all, nothing to worry about. What is all the commotion downstairs?"

Sarah reached for a blue robe draped across the bedpost. "Get up, it's your folks. They returned with your wedding trousseau—boxes and boxes. Oh my! There will be fittings and inventory. You must get up. Don't let them catch ya still abed."

"Oh, my gosh, my wedding trousseau…they're home. I can't wait to see what they bought."

"What change of heart is this? Last night's dinner was that good was it? Did Mrs. Kirby put some potion in yer food to make ya change your mind?"

"Well, no, I mean, no…I don't want to marry, but Peter is a likeable sort, and Mrs. Kirby is very entertaining. You know as well as I do, when Mother makes up her mind about something, there is no turning her around. So, I might as well accept it, make the most of it. Besides, think of all the new clothes. You know I can't resist new clothes." She turned around in the front of the mirror laughing.

Sarah walked to the doorway. "You best be careful, Miss. Your mother won't know what to make of your sudden compliance to her wishes. She'll think you've somethin' up your sleeve." Sarah descended the stairs in response to Mrs. Squire's summons.

Mother sounds jovial enough. I don't hear Papa. I wonder what he really thinks of all this.

The large clock on her dresser chimed the hour.

Eight o'clock! My goodness, I should've been up an hour ago. The blue robe landed on the floor, and she ran to the closet to find a dress. She wiggled into the navy blue housedress, brushed her hair, and swept it up into a ponytail. After a hasty toilet, she gave her hair one last pat, and walked slowly down the stairs. "Sarah's right. I must not be too agreeable. Peter warned me, too."

"Mother, Father, you're home. How was your trip?"

"What are you doing out of your room, Ruth? I told Sarah to keep you in there while we were away."

Ruth smiled. For some reason, she assumed Mother would look different, less severe. Alas no, still the same plain dress, her hair again pulled sharply back in an unflattering bun, an ever-present scowl a permanent fixture on her face. "I have been in my room, Mother. But you're home now, surely you trust me enough to come and greet you and Father."

Priscilla Squire's frown deepened, but she nodded her approval. "Well, I suppose you may have a little freedom, now. Nevertheless, don't try anything, young lady. You'll be married in a month, and I'll hear no more about it."

"As you wish, Mother. Remember, I've met Mrs. Kirby. She is very kind and helped me see the error of my ways. I'll not fight you on the matter."

"Well, at last, you are showing some sense. Mrs. Kirby is a lovely woman with a good head on her shoulders. I can only hope she will have a positive influence on you. I certainly haven't."

Ruth looked around for Father, but only saw the door of his study close behind him. *He's not speaking to me. He's either angry or sad. I wish I could speak to him alone.*

The two delivery men teetered under the load of the boxes, bounced off the doorway, but finally managed to deposit the last of the cargo on the floor of the parlor.

"Oh goodie, I can't wait to see what's in the boxes," Ruth squealed.

"Stop at once, Ruth. I must organize things. You will not try them on or fuss with them until I tell you. Is that clear?"

"But Mother, how will I know if they suit me? Have I no say in anything?"

"Ah, I see rebellion is still prominent. I was beginning to wonder what came over you. I'll have them sorted out and hung in the guest room in short order. You can wait until then."

When she heard *guest room*, she froze. *Do I want my wedding clothes anywhere near that room?* Maybe what happened in the guest room was like a premonition, a version of herself getting ready for her wedding. When she thought of it that way, she relaxed, and began to think she imagined the whole thing, dreamed it. "What shall I do in the mean time, Mother?"

Mrs. Squire paused at the foot of the stairs, a large box in her arms. "I want you to help Sarah. The crystal needs cleaning. The house needs to be put in order for the guests and parties, and Sarah can't do it alone. It will keep you occupied and out of trouble. Besides, you will need to get use to caring for your own home and belongings. I doubt very much Mrs. Kirby has a maid."

Mrs. Squire turned her back. Ruth frowned and made a face at her retreating matriarch. Left alone in the foyer, she shrugged and turned for the kitchen. "Mother says the crystal needs to be cleaned, and I'm to help you, Sarah. I must say, a cloud of gloom always precedes Mother's arrival."

"Now, Ruth, you mustn't speak ill of your ma. She has your future to think of, remember. Come, I'll show you what to do."

They found Mr. Squire in the hallway looking around like a lost puppy.

"Father, what's wrong, what are you doing?"

"Where is your mother?"

"Upstairs, putting boxes away in the guest room."

He began to climb the stairs. "The bank called. They want to talk to us. I knew we spent too much on this wedding."

Sarah grabbed Ruth's hand. "Come, we have crystal to clean."

One by one, they removed the numerous pieces of precious glass from the antique china cabinet. She almost forgot about her parents until she heard them arguing in the hall. Together, they entered the dining room, and Ruth was startled by the look on Father's face.

"Ruth, Sarah, we are going to town for awhile. Continue what you're doing, and when you're finished, start on the silver," Mother said.

Before either girl could answer, the Squires grabbed their coats, and slammed the door behind them.

◆◆◆◆

"Good morning, Mr. and Mrs. Squire. It was good of you to come on such short notice. There is a matter we must discuss, and I am afraid it is of dire urgency."

Eric Horton stood as the Squires entered his office, moved around behind them, and closed the door. His quarters were small, no windows…warm, cluttered, and there was a musty smell. The exception was the surface of his desk where lay one single sheet of paper. They took their seats where indicated, and he moved back behind his desk, and sat down.

Mrs. Squire cradled a large, brown leather purse on her lap, back straight, a deep scowl on her face. "I do not know what is so urgent, Mr. Horton. We are just back from New York and not quite settled yet."

Eric sat back in his comfortable chair, aligned his fingers together on each hand like a web, and assumed his well-practiced condescending attitude. "Exactly…New York. How is it possible you can afford a trip to New York City, pray tell?"

Priscilla sat up straighter, and her face grew red. "I beg your pardon, Mr. Horton? What business is that of yours?" She stood and pushed her chair backwards. "How dare you."

"It is my business, Mrs. Squire, because you are in default on your house loan. I am afraid I must issue a foreclosure."

Her gasp was audible, and Robert Squire half stood from his chair as he caught his wife in mid fall. He helped her settle into the chair and stood awkwardly, for a moment, before he returned to his seat.

"I see this has taken you by surprise, Mrs. Squire. Surely, you were aware of the increase in your payment and the growing interest. Have you not discussed this with your husband?" Eric looked from one to the other, triumphant.

Priscilla regained her composure. She sat up straighter and looked squarely into Eric Horton's eyes. "You cannot do this to us at this particular time. We have everything planned. Yes, I knew about the increase. I kept it from my husband. He is a writer, and I knew if I told him, it would block his ability to write. He has not sold his work as regular as before, and we have drifted behind a bit. Naturally, as long standing customers, we assumed you would let us find a way to catch up. Please Mr. Horton."

Eric leaned forward in his chair and addressed her alone. "I pride myself in keeping personal feelings out of my business decisions, Mrs. Squire. I like both of you, very much. It is against my better judgment to let it go this long. Now, you are in default, and there is little I can do, except…"

"Except what, Mr. Horton?" Her voice dripped with disdain.

Eric suppressed a satisfied smile. *Ah, now she is ready to listen.* "I am at a time in my life when I must consider a step up in my profession. There are certain expectations from my peers and superiors which must be fulfilled in order to climb the ladder, so to speak, in this industry," he began.

Mrs. Squire waved her hand. "Yes, yes, Mr. Horton. What has that got to with my husband and I—and our mortgage?"

He lowered his glasses on the bridge of his nose and looked over the top. "If you would allow me to finish, I believe it will become clear what it has to do with you, Mrs. Squire."

She sat back in her chair with a sigh, crossed her ankles, and cocked her head.

"As I was saying, I want a promotion, and I want to improve my lifestyle. I have worked hard to get where I am and am ready for the next level. In order to achieve that level, certain things are required. It must look as if I am improving myself. I have found a lovely home in the better district in town. I can afford it very easily, but it lacks a certain *accrouement*. There is also another requirement for the next step in my career. The powers that be judge your character, and your ability to conduct responsible business, by this standard."

Priscilla uncrossed her ankles. "What standard, Mr. Horton?"

"A wife, Mrs. Squire. They require I be married," he stated.

Mr. Squire looked up from his lap and stared at Eric.

"Well, it should not be too hard to acquire, Mr. Horton, for a man of your means," Priscilla replied.

Mr. Squire spoke for the first time. "Wife, you do not understand Mr. Horton's meaning. He wants a wife; our daughter to be exact. Correct, Horton?"

"Correct, Mr. Squire. I am glad to see how astute you are in catching my meaning. I want to marry your daughter. If we can make it happen, I'll be willing to overlook your foreclosure, and maybe pay off the loan entirely. I know she is only seventeen, young and inexperienced, but I am a man of the world. I can teach her to be a lady."

Mrs. Squire struggled to her feet. She wavered a little, but found her balance. "You are saying you want to marry my Ruth, and you will dismiss the foreclosure, and see to it the loan is paid in full?"

"Yes, that about sums it up. I think it is a reasonable deal, Mrs. Squire. I realize arranged marriages are a thing of the past, a relic of the old country, but it *is* still done on occasion."

"She cannot marry you. Not *you!* She is engaged to be married in a month. That is why we went to New York, to buy her trousseau. She is spoken for, Mr. Horton."

Eric stood up and faced her. "Married? How could she be getting married? I have not seen her with anyone. I move in the best circles, I would have heard about it. Who? Do I know him? Can we buy him off? She is the only one I have considered. She is beautiful and would compliment me to perfection. I would be assured of getting the promotion."

"She is engaged to Peter Kirby. I am sure you do not know him. He is much younger than you, and they are a very good match."

Eric Horton sat down with a thud. "Did you say Peter Kirby? Tall, blond young man?"

"Yes, do you know him?"

"I met him this morning. He tried to open a household account for his new bride. I had no idea it was my Ruth."

Priscilla laughed. "She is not *your* Ruth."

Eric focused his attention, once more, squarely on Mrs. Squire. "I suggest you *make* her my Ruth, if you know what is good for you. Either she becomes my wife, and you get rid of Peter Kirby, or you will find yourself homeless, as well as penniless. Are we clear?"

"Are you threatening us, Mr. Horton? Because, if you are, I shall obtain a lawyer. You have hit my husband and me with quite an ultimatum. There is so much more to consider than this one thing. I implore you to give us a day or two to digest your request. You can not expect us to give you an answer on such short notice."

"I can see where this might have come as a surprise to you, but I suggest you dismiss the idea of a lawyer. I am well within my legal right to foreclose. I know people, Mrs. Squire, people who can make your life miserable. Be in my office in two days at nine o'clock, and we will discuss this further. I will want to call on Ruth in the afternoon and express my desire to wed her."

"Come, Robert, we need to go," Priscilla said.

Eric came around the desk and opened the office door. He called to them as they walked out into the foyer. "Remember, two days, nine o'clock." A maniacal grin formed on his lips as he watched them leave. "They have no choice but to bow to my wishes. Therefore, Peter Kirby, you will not need the household account. Your good looks will not help you out this time."

◆◆◆◆

Ruth and Sarah polished the silver in silence. The crystal gleamed, and they finished the last set of silver trays.

"Do you think I am pretty, Sarah. I mean, pretty enough to attract a man?" Ruth turned to and fro admiring her reflection in the large tray.

"You've already attracted a man, silly. What are you worried about?" the maid replied.

Ruth replaced the tray on the shelf. "He doesn't really have a choice in the matter, Sarah. Does he really think I am pretty, or is he settling for what he can get?"

Sarah handed another tray to Ruth. "Are ya serious, girl? Have ya not seen the way he looks at you? There is no doubt he thinks yer pretty. He fair can not keep his hands off of you."

They were both laughing when her parents came through the door.

"How was your trip to the bank, Mother? Did you see that horrid Mr. Horton?" Ruth called.

"Keep to your work and leave the business to your parents, Ruth. Your father and I will be upstairs. We do not want to be disturbed."

Mother's voice was harsh, but what Ruth noticed the most was her red nose and red-rimmed eyes. Father marched upstairs behind his wife.

"What was that all about, Sarah?"

"I certainly do not know, nor is it any of my business. Don't bother your head about it. I am sure your parents have everything under control." Sarah finished the last piece, gathered her supplies, and started for the kitchen.

"Don't leave me, Sarah. Something is wrong. I can feel it. What shall I do? Sit in my room?"

"Exactly what I would do. No sense in causing upheaval right now. Best you let them take the lead. I'll come up in a while after I make sure dinner is okay."

Ruth nodded and made her way slowly up the stairs. The closer she got to the top, the more she thought heard voices. She crept up the stairs and fought the urge to inch toward her mother's door. Instead, she turned into her room and shut the door. She shook off a chill, but a sense of foreboding crept into her bones.

◆◆◆◆

"You cannot possibly consider marrying our beautiful daughter to horrible Mr. Horton, Priscilla. It is vulgar and unconscionable. She did nothing to deserve such a fate." Robert Squire faced his wife for the first time, in a long while. Content to let her run the show, he lost touch, and now, found the household out of control.

"Don't you think I know what it will do to her? Robert, what choice do we have? Horton boxed us into a corner. We will lose everything. He threatened us. If I let my mind wander, I can imagine him in the middle of The Purple Gang or worse. He is that corrupt! We might need to fear for our safety and Ruth's, also."

"If only you told me what was happening." He threw his hat on the four-poster bed. "Heaven forbid no, it must be your way every time and look at the mess you created."

Priscilla whirled to face him, arms akimbo, eyes bulging. "My way? You blame this on me? You…who sits in his office all evening, writing his pathetic stories, while I juggle the household finances, figure out how to keep food on the table, and clothes on our backs. Do you think the house runs itself? Never once did you ask about anything to do with this house. You take no interest in this family except to spoil Ruth. And now you want to judge me?" Tears coursed down her cheeks.

Robert sat down hard on the bed, bowed his head. After a moment, the tears tore at his heart, and he rose, crossed the room, and wiped them away. "My dear, I do not mean to judge you, but sensed for a long time you find me inadequate. We grew apart and no longer talk to one another. I suppose my withdrawal put more of a burden on you, but in recent years, the light-hearted girl I married disappeared. You are so severe and cold." He walked to the window and stared at the grounds below. "I wonder, at times, if you wish you married Alexander, instead of me. Maybe you made a hasty decision under the circumstances. Things are very wrong with us, Priscilla. Ruth deserves loving parents, and we are not anymore."

The room was quiet as a church, the only sound, the ticking of the wooden clock on the night table.

Priscilla shuffled her feet, moved forward, and touched his hand. "Robert, I…I did not know you felt this way. Maybe I turned a bit sour over the years. But, Alexander? Marry him?" She shook her head. "How could you entertain such an idea? He could not hold a candle to you. It was you who stole my heart with your passionate rhetoric on the problems of the day—your ability to articulate precisely a point that needed to be made. You wooed my heart with your words, your kindness, your acceptance of the unsavory situation. Alexander was a rake and a scoundrel. Alexander, indeed." She walked toward the bed.

He followed her. "Never mind all that now, it's water under the bridge. A much bigger problem looms before us. What shall we do about this situation?"

She reached out and squeezed his hand. "We have no choice, Robert. We need to call off the marriage between Peter and Ruth, and get her betrothed to Eric Horton, or we will lose everything."

"No! I accept no part in marrying our only child off to the likes of him. These problems are of our making. She should not suffer for them."

She took the other hand. "Robert, please…be sensible. Eric has more money. Besides, Peter has his mother and two brothers still to care for—what of them? How well off will Ruth be married to him with all his responsibility? I didn't want to mention it before, but Peter's last name is Kirby. Is he connected to the Kirby gang in the city? I know he came from the old country, but do we really know? With Eric, she will live in a grand house, own plenty of clothes, and secure a place in society. Surely, you can see the sense of this. Yes, we made mistakes, but would Ruth be better off married to the milkman? Really? The corruption in the city worries me. If Eric is connected to unsavory people, Ruth might be safer married to him."

Robert felt confused, defeated. "I don't know any more, Priscilla. It is beyond my ability to sort it out. I will go with whatever you decide." He walked to the door, put his hand on the knob, and turned back to his wife. "I will not be party to breaking this news to her. I cannot bear to see her cry." He slammed the door as he left, and the noise echoed down the hall.

Chapter Ten

The earthy smell of grass and dirt filled Elizabeth's nostrils and reminded her of home. She sat back on her heels to rest her sore knees and stiff back. The long, muslin skirt caught on the heel of one shoe. She fell back and rolled onto the ground. Unhurt, she laughed at her clumsiness and brushed the dirt from her backside. "Elizabeth, old girl, you are not quite as spry as in your younger days. Maybe it's time I called it a day in the garden. Spring is in my veins, I want my beds to be ready, but the boys will be home soon. I must clean up and prepare dinner for my hungry mob."

A cloud of dust blossomed as her dirty hands brushed the rumpled skirt to remove the last remnants of the flowerbed. Satisfaction warmed her heart on this day. She began to hum on the way to the house. *My oldest son is going to marry a lovely girl. His business is growing and doing well. The two youngest boys are healthy, robust, and excelling in school. Life has taken a turn for the better for me since my husband's death. I am truly blessed.*

She turned the corner of the house surprised to see a black taxicab parked in her drive. *Funny…I didn't hear anyone pull in the drive, and I wasn't expecting anyone. Wonder who it can be?* Curious, she walked toward the car.

"Over here, Mrs. Kirby. I am over here." A young, fair-haired woman, dressed in a long, somber, black dress, perched on the porch swing.

"Oh hello, I'm sorry. If you knocked, I am afraid I was in the back, in my garden. May I help you with something?"

The woman stood and reached out a hand in greeting. Tall and slender with a plain face, she reached out a hand. "Yes, you may. I would like to come in and converse with you. My journey was long and would plead with you for refreshment, if you don't mind."

"Certainly, I'm afraid my hands are dirty from all the digging. Come in and sit in the parlor while I clean up a bit." Elizabeth went to the door and pulled it open with a gesture for the woman to come inside.

"Very well. That suits me exactly."

The two women entered the house, and Elizabeth showed her into the parlor. "I'll only be a minute, Miss. I'm sorry, but I did not get your name."

"Hattie, my name is Hattie Morgenstern."

Elizabeth gave the woman a nod. "Hattie, please sit down, make yourself at home. I'll wash up and bring tea. "

"You're very kind," the woman said.

Mrs. Kirby smiled and left to clean up. While she washed her hands, changed to a fresh apron, and jammed another pin into errant locks, the nagging notion plagued her. *The name sounds so familiar. For the life of me, I cannot place put my finger on it. She looks to be around Peter's age.*

Presentable again, she carried the tea tray into the parlor laden with teacakes and her company china cups. She set them on the small table in front of the girl. "Now, Miss Morgenstern, let me pour the tea.

Please help yourself to the cakes. I made them fresh this morning."

Hattie Morgenstern devoured a cake with one bite. "They are scrumptious. You smell of mint, Mrs. Kirby. Do you have a spice garden in the back?"

The delicate teacup rattled as she poured. "Actually, I do. Gardening is my passion. I use the spices in all my recipes and baffle the locals with the flavors. I brought them from my homeland. My sons, at least, can enjoy the taste of home. The mint is from a mix for the tea. I guess that is why you noticed it. What brings you to the Kirbys, Hattie? May I call you by your first name? You seem so familiar." Elizabeth settled back in her chair and sipped her tea. She studied the young woman's proper black dress and her manner; the way she sat…so straight and crossed her ankles.

Hattie dabbed her rosebud mouth with Elizabeth's fine linen napkin and returned her hands to her lap. "What brings me here, Mrs. Kirby, is the necessity to fulfill the contract between you and me."

Elizabeth stopped the advance of her teacup to her lips. "Contract? What contract, Miss Morgenstern? I don't believe I have ever laid eyes on you before, although, you do seem familiar. What is this all about?" She set her cup down and leaned forward.

"The marriage contract. The one you and your husband signed at my birth and of your son's. Peter, isn't it?"

Stunned, Elizabeth couldn't move. Her mouth fell open. All she could do was continue to stare at the girl.

"Mrs. Kirby? Are you all right? You look a bit surprised. May I get you something—a drink of water perhaps?"

The beautiful, sunny day, the birds singing in the trees, the glorious earthy smell as she puttered in the flowerbeds, the complete sense of peace and serenity shattered at once. The contract. It came rushing back to her like a lightning bolt from a cloudless sky.

Of course, how could she forget? The old days…when marriages were arranged between households to ensure family lines. At birth, parents would align themselves with a family of prominence to betroth their children to each other, thus assuring the security of the family name. She and her husband followed the custom without question when Peter was born. Over the years, times changed, the world became more modern, and the tradition, although not completely abandoned, was not adhered to as rigidly. Certainly, this woman would not hold her to such an archaic promise.

She poured a bit more tea, rearranged the cakes on the tray, gathered her thoughts, and tried not to project panic. "Yes, Mrs. Morgenstern, I do remember the old contract, but it was a long time ago, another country, another time. Surely, you do not suggest we honor such an outdated tradition, in this new age. What of your family, where are they?'

Hattie Morgenstern trained her gaze on Elizabeth. Her voice remained steady, without a trace of a waver as she answered. "My family is all gone, died in an accident. I am alone in this world. From a little girl, my mother told me of the agreement between our two families, and of Peter. I have dreamed about him all my life. I always knew he would be my husband. I only have pictures of him as a boy. Of course, you remember the village gatherings our families attended. Unfortunately, things changed. You moved to another village, and for a while, my parents kept track of where you lived. I believe your husband passed a way a few years ago, and my family met with misfortune resulting in their deaths. I have no one—nothing but this contract. So, you see, I intend to have it honored, Mrs. Kirby." She pulled a rolled piece of paper from her cloak and presented it to Elizabeth.

Unable to blink, Elizabeth took the paper, untied the bow, and read the printed words of the agreement of the betrothal. She saw her very own signature on the bottom of the scroll, and her heart sank. The paper became a heavy stone in her hands, and she lowered it to her lap, but Hattie reached over and snatched it back. "Hattie, I understand your plight and will truly help you in any way I can. Your mother and father were friends of mine, and I am so sorry to hear of their fate. The thing is, we cannot honor this contract, for you see, Peter is engaged to someone else. They are to be married in a few weeks. This situation cannot happen."

Hattie Morgenstern stood abruptly and pulled herself to her full height. "Mrs. Kirby, I suggest you find a way out of his engagement, because I intend to hold you to your commitment if I have to take it to the law. I have taken residence at Mrs. Whitewood's Boarding House. I will be back this evening to speak with Peter and suggest you make him aware of his responsibility. Good day, madam."

Miss Morgenstern was out the door and into the waiting cab before Elizabeth could stop her. Elizabeth Kirby fell back into her chair, panic rising in her throat. *Peter will be home in an hour, what in God's name am I to say to him?*

Chapter Eleven

Ruth had never seen Mother so undone. Mrs. Squire's hair was frazzled, her eyes wild, as if she were afraid. They sat in the sun porch, alone. *Mother said she wanted to talk to me. What is she up to now? How I wish I could see Peter. Maybe that's it. We are going to set up dinner with the entire family. I suppose I can't let her know I don't find the prospect of marriage to Peter all that distasteful, anymore. That would make her too happy.*

"Please sit down. There is something I need to discuss with you." Priscilla Squire tugged the sleeve of Ruth's dress, and they sat down on the cold wooden bench.

Defiance returned in the face of her feelings for Peter. "What is it Mother, more plans, more ways to make me suffer? Oh, Peter is pleasant enough, but I told you, I do not want to marry. Not him, not anyone."

Mrs. Squire took both Ruth's hands and looked at her in earnest. "You will not marry Peter Kirby, my dear."

Ruth's breath caught for an instant. *Did I hear Mother correctly? Not marry Peter?* A sudden stab of disappointment zipped through frayed nerve endings. "What do you mean? Did you see the harshness of this punishment? You and Father came to your senses? What of Peter, does he know this, yet?"

Mrs. Squire dropped her daughter's hands and looked out at nothing, a blank stare on her face. "No, Peter does not know. I will go to the Kirby's in the morning. I did not say you would not marry, Ruth. You will not marry Peter."

It took a moment for her words to penetrate. *Not marry Peter? But ... someone? Who?* "You found another husband for me? Am I to be auctioned off to the highest bidder? Who is he, Mother?"

Priscilla stared at her hands in her lap. "Eric Horton."

Silence filled the air. Ruth could not speak much less breathe. The name her mother spewed out was like a slap. It could not be.

"The banker?" She managed. "The banker, Mother?"

"Yes, Mr. Horton, the banker."

"No! I will not. He is horrible—fat and ugly. You cannot mean you want me to spend my life with such a toad."

"You will do as you are told, Ruth. It is a very good match. He is getting a promotion, buying a new house in the wealthy district. You will be in society, enjoy security. You will be the envy of Detroit's elite, and you will get used to him. He will be kind to you."

Ruth balled both fists, her eyes bulged, and her voice took on a low guttural tone. "You will never get me to marry the likes of Eric Horton, Mother. If you do, I will never forgive you or Father. You cannot do this to me. There must be laws."

"I *can* do this, Ruth. You are underage and lean toward unacceptable behavior. Any court would uphold my decision."

A sob wrenched through Ruth, and she ran from the porch. *I will not marry Mr. Horton. I don't know how, but I will get away from here. Father...I must find him. He won't allow this. He's a fair man, a loving man. More importantly, he loves me and would want me to be happy. But wait – maybe Father doesn't know. This is all Mother's idea.* The back door slammed, and one shoe flew off her foot on the way up the stairs. It did not matter. Sobs wracked her body, and she fell in a heap in front of his bedroom door. One hand rose weakly to knock, but the door swung open, and her daddy filled the doorframe.

He scooped her up in both arms like a child. "Oh, Ruthie, my Ruthie, my sweet little girl. I do not know what to do or how to help you. I am so sorry. It is all my fault, my fault." He buried his face in her hair.

"Father, she wants me to marry the banker, Mr. Horton. Why? What is the matter with Peter? Father, why is it your fault? What is going on? Don't tell me you *knew* about this."

He brushed the tousled curls from her face. She settled on his knee as he sat on the edge of the bed. "Daughter, these things are bigger than your seventeen years need to worry about. I knew, Ruthie, but I don't condone it. Mother thinks there is no other way."

"But, it is *my* life, Father. Don't I have a right to know, when it is I who suffers?"

He pushed her from his lap and walked to the window. "You are right, of course. Horton is foreclosing on the house, Ruth. Our payments are out of hand, and we have no recourse. If we agree to give him your hand in marriage, he will take care of the problem."

She followed him to the window. "So, I am to be a payment to keep the house. I am to save this family?"

He turned from the window. "You must leave, Ruth. You must go and find Peter. This is not right; you must not be involved in our failures. Go to Peter, and tell him what is happening. Maybe he will marry you right away. So what if we lose the house? With you married, your mother and I can live in an apartment in town. A new beginning may be what we need. It could be just what I need to find my muse once more." He pushed her toward the door and shut it behind her.

How was she to get to Peter? Would he want her when he found out about all this? The hallway was dark. She took a halting step, stopped, and looked back toward her father's bedroom door.

"Ruthie," someone whispered in the darkness.

She jumped and peered into the dark passageway. "Who is it?"

"Come with me, Ruthie, quickly," the voice whispered again.

"Sarah? Is that you?"

"Yes, now come along, quickly before your mother finds you." The maid reached out, grabbed her hand, and pulled her toward Mother's bedroom door.

Irritated, Ruth tried to withdraw. "What are you doing? She will find me in there. You know she never wants me to set foot in her room. I cannot go in there while she's home, Sarah."

"Yes, you can. It is exactly the last place she will think to look. In the closet, Ruth."

"The … the closet. Where I found the letters?"

Sarah pulled Ruth into the forbidden boudoir. "There is no time. Come, she will be here any moment."

They stumbled across the room where Sarah grabbed the glass doorknob, pushed Ruth through the door, and followed behind her. It was dark, and Ruth could not see her own hand in front of her face.

Sarah pushed past the younger woman, took her hand, and led her to the end of the closet. When they turned the corner, Ruth could see light peek through under the door connected to the guest room. The illumination was enough for Ruth to see the same ball gowns and jewelry as before. *They weren't my imagination.*

"Sarah, did you know about these…?"

"Not now, Ruth. There's not much time." They turned the corner, and Sarah laid a hand on the knob, but hesitated. "Before we go in, Ruth, you must know, but be patient, and I'll explain, only right now, we have to escape your mother."

Ruth pulled back and stood rigid. "Wait Sarah, won't she find us in the guest room? She might already be in there, for all we know."

"Hush, we're not going in the guest room. This closet is a secret room. Your mother doesn't know it exists. She gave me those letters to burn. I didn't…instead, I hid them here. My intention was to keep them hidden forever, and never allow you to find out. There is no choice now. If I am to save you from Eric Horton, you must remain here. I never lied to you or led you astray, have I? Our friendship started the day you were born. Will you trust me?"

Ruth relaxed her shoulders. "Yes, I cannot imagine what is going on, but if it will save me from Eric Horton, the choice is made."

Sarah led Ruth to the white vanity and pointed to the matching stool. "Sit." The room was aglow with soft shadow thrown from an antique globe lamp. "Be quiet. I will explain later." She opened the lower drawer of the vanity and pulled out a picture album, along with more letters tied in ribbons. "Now, I have to go. They will miss me. I'll return in a while. Don't leave this room, understand?"

"But…" Ruth began.

"No buts. We will talk when I get back. Now behave." Sarah left through the closet door.

Ruth looked at the album, opened it carefully, and stared in disbelief.

Chapter Twelve

The day's route ended without incident. Tired and frustrated, Peter was anxious to get home. Doubts invaded his mind, repeatedly, troubled his thoughts, and distracted him from work. *Maybe she is too young. Maybe this is unfair for her. Yes, there is a strong attraction, but at seventeen, how can she really know?*

The horses came to a stop outside the small barn, and in mechanical fashion, the night's routine was accomplished. He brushed them down, put out the feed, secured the wagon for the next day, and headed toward the welcoming light in the window.

An unsettling sensation overcame him in the empty kitchen. *Something is not quite right…no warm aroma of a promised meal Where are my brothers*? He called out, "Mother?" Cruel silence added to the confusion, an ominous companion. *The garden, she could be out there. Could she have fallen or worse?* The moonless evening inhibited the search, but he tore through the winter cabbage, the purple-sprouting Brussels sprouts, and carrots with little care of her faithful tending, even in the cold season. Only the faint bark of a distant dog answered his frantic cries. *She must be in the house.*

He found her in the parlor, in a chair, hair mussed, and a frightened look etched on her face. Alarm heightened by her disheveled appearance, he spoke softly, "Mother, what is it? What has happened? Are you hurt? Is it the boys? Where are they?"

Elizabeth turned a dazed stare toward Peter. "They are at the neighbors down the road. I had to send them there for a while."

He took her hand gently. "Why, has something happened? Please tell me. My heart is beating out of my chest."

She sat up a bit straighter and withdrew her hand. "Yes, something has happened. Sit down, and I will try to explain."

Peter rose, seated himself on the settee opposite her, and gave his full attention. "Please, Mother. I am listening."

"I had a visitor this morning."

"Okay, a visitor. Was it a man or a woman?"

"It was a young woman. A Hattie Morgenstern … from the home country." A lifeless silence filled the room.

"Well, it must have been pleasant for you, a visitor from home. The name sounds vaguely familiar. Why did she come, why is her visit upsetting you so?"

Elizabeth shifted in the chair. "I knew her. She was born a short while after you. Our families were close neighbors."

He drew a ragged breath, impatient. "Well, how nice you could see her again, all grown up. Get to the point, Mother. What did she want?"

"To marry you, Peter. She is your true betrothed."

The room spun. *What did Mother say—my true betrothed?*

"Let me start at the beginning. It is a long story." Elizabeth relayed the tale of his birth and the customs of the day, while he listened, stunned.

Thirty minutes later, Peter stood, fists clenched at his side. "How dare she! An ancient contract between two people who have never met? I have something to say about this, Mother, and I won't be forced into a marriage by anyone. Ruth and I are engaged. I came home to tell you. We talked last night, and I realized she finds me desirable, after all. We have a true connection, and I will not give up my engagement to Ruth for this other woman."

Elizabeth stood up slowly. "Peter, it is not so different from what we arranged between you and Ruth. Don't you see? This woman lost her whole family. There is no one and nowhere to go. She intends to take legal action if we do not honor the contract. What are we to do, Peter? Miss Morgenstern is coming back this evening to speak with you."

"She is what?" He paced the floor. "I will not. I want nothing to do with her. Let her try to involve the law. It will never be considered in an American court."

"Peter, please, at least meet with her. She is all alone. Maybe we can work something out. Help her find a new life in this country."

"No, Mother. I won't be here when she arrives. I'm going to find Ruth. You can deal with Hattie Morgenstern. You and Father signed the contract, not me. It is your responsibility to set things right. She better be gone when I get back." He started for the door, but turned and looked at his mother again. "For the first time in my life I feel happy, excited to have found someone who makes my soul soar. I cannot turn it off to honor some stupid contract you signed twenty-seven years ago." The door slammed behind him.

Furious, he drove recklessly down the country road. The willow tree where he kissed Ruth came into view, and he slowed down. The recent memory made his body yearn, the heat of desire almost unbearable.

He pressed his foot harder on the gas pedal and sped toward town. The intention was to take Ruth this very minute, find somewhere to marry, and end this nonsense. At the cross roads, before the entrance to the city, an automobile sat crooked on the side of the road. Even in the dark, the flat tire was obvious. *A taxi, but what of the woman standing beside it? She's alone…not a good situation.* He pulled to the curb. "Is there something I can do to help?" The woman lowered the hood from her cloak, and he caught his breath. "Sarah, what are you doing out here?"

"Oh Master Peter, you are the one I was coming to see. Please, I need to speak to you. It is very urgent. We need to go at once." She ran to his car.

"Is Ruth all right? Is she hurt?" He opened the car door and stood beside the little maid.

She grabbed the lapels of his overcoat. "Safe for the moment, sir. Something has happened. I had to hide her. You must save her from a fate worse than death."

"I will go at once, but wait…do you need help, sir?" Peter called to cabbie.

The driver shook his head. "I'll tell you what, mister. I am glad to get this woman away from me. To hear her tell it, it is a matter of life and death. The flat—I drove too fast. It just blew. Take her and be done with it. I can change a tire. Thanks anyway." The man reached into the back of the motorcar, withdrew a jack, turned his back on the couple, and set to work.

Relieved, Peter turned to Sarah. "Get in, you can tell me what happened on the way to town." He opened the passenger door and helped her inside. Settled behind the wheel, Peter engaged the engine. "Start at the beginning, Sarah. Tell me everything."

As the car sped along, Sarah told Peter about the dark, sinister situation with Eric Horton.

When she finished the story, Peter remained silent. *Eric Horton. I was in his bank yesterday and listened to the greasy man speak of marriage. To picture him with my Ruth is beyond comprehension.* His foot pressed hard on the pedal, once more.

"You must park down the block, Mr. Kirby. You cannot let them see you. It would not do for them to find you," Sarah cautioned.

Peter nodded. "Yes, you're right. Where is she in the house? Can you show me?"

"Yes, follow me, and we will go through the back way. Be very quiet.

They huddled together and walked down the block while Sarah explained the secret room. To think, only a week ago, he was content to drive the milk route, and tend to Mother and his two brothers, without a care in the world. Now …

Sarah turned the key in the backdoor lock and held a finger to her lips. He acknowledged the sign with a nod.

A back stairway, once used by servants, led upstairs to the bedrooms and came out near Robert Kirby's bedroom. If careful, they could make it past the door without detection.

"I need to find out where Mrs. Squire is, Peter. If she is in her room, we will have to wait until morning. Let me go and see what I can find. You wait here, in the old stairway, until I come back." She pushed him into a dark corner and left to find Ruth's mother.

Peter was uncomfortable standing like a thief, hiding. Yes, Sarah let him in, but she was only the maid, not the owners of the domain. *They might consider it breaking and entering if I am caught.* He shuffled from one foot to the other, impatient for her return. After an eternity, soft footsteps echoed in the hall.

"Mrs. Squire is in the parlor, crying. We can go up these stairs, undetected, but you must be careful, the steps are treacherous." Sarah lit a candle and led the way. Peter followed, cautious, testing each step before he put his weight on the board.

They came to the last step without mishap, but when Sarah tried the door, it would not budge. "She locked it. Wait here, I'll go down and fetch the key." Her small frame wedged past him.

Peter waited, palms damp, skin crawling, trapped in the dark like an animal. Forever passed before she returned, key in hand.

Once the door was unlocked, Sarah poked her head out to survey the hallway. She grabbed Peter's hand and pulled him down the hall. They stopped in front of Mrs. Squire's bedroom door.

"We have to go through the closet to get to the secret room. Be very quiet, Peter."

They tiptoed into the room, and Sarah opened the closet door.

Peter pulled back a bit. "It is pitch black in here. What have you gotten me in to, there's no one here."

Sarah tugged his hand. "Please, Peter, we have to get to the back of the closet. Come."

He drew in his breath, set his jaw, and prepared for the worst. If this was a trap, he wanted to be ready to fight.

The closet ended, but Sarah moved forward again and disappeared behind a corner. Peter followed. All of a sudden, he saw a light ahead of him. The closet was full of fancy gowns, shoes, and jewelry, the likes of which he'd never seen before. He stayed close behind the maid.

She came to the door and looked back at him. "She's in there."

The door opened, and he saw Ruth perched on the white vanity, open letters in her lap. Tears streamed down her cheeks. He forgot the need to speak softly and blurted, "Ruth, are you all right?"

She gasped, stumbled into his arms, and sobbed, "Oh, Peter, I thought I would never see you again."

"It's all right now, I'm here. We are going to sort this all out." His arms tightened around her.

Ruth clung to Peter.

Sarah cleared her throat and whispered, "Did you read the letters, my child? See the pictures?"

Ruth pulled away from Peter. "Yes, it's unbelievable. Mother was a spoiled brat and never really loved Father. I will never forgive her … never!"

Chapter Thirteen

Priscilla Squire sat in the parlor alone, the lace handkerchief wet with tears. Every fiber of her body screamed she should find Ruth, but her energy was sapped, all strength gone…defeated. Robert blamed her, and Ruth hated her. *I've made so many mistakes, taken so many wrong turns, and now, I've made my daughter suffer for my own transgressions.* The room was a warm inviting place, and she scanned it slowly, absorbing every inch as if it was the last time she would see her beloved sanctuary. What was she to do? Force wouldn't persuade Ruth to marry Eric Horton. Peter was, by far, the better choice for her happiness. *What of the house, our home since I was a baby? What of my husband, what will become of us?*

She paced the floor, went to the window, and moved the curtain aside as if an answer would fly through to save them. It didn't, and the heavy drape dropped back into place. *No, I must face this music alone. Where is Ruth, now? Probably in Robert's room seeking comfort. They are so close. Ruth loves him more than me. Well, I should not be surprised. All I wanted was for her to have more out of life.*

Seated on the settee again, she thought of the days of her young womanhood. *So many suitors, so many choices. There was Edward. Very handsome, wanted to be a lawyer…and Alexander…I thought he was the love of my life. We danced together at the cotillions and the balls. He was a perfect dancer, and I, the candy on his arm.* For a moment, she could see the girl again, and tears sprang to her eyes at the memory of that horrible night.

It was the night of the All City Ball. There were several gowns to choose from, and she could not make up her mind. Sarah nipped and tucked each one to help her make a decision, and finally settled on the rose. Or rather, Sarah settled on it. Red was her first choice, but it wasn't allowed.

As it turned out, Sarah's choice was perfect. All the attention was on her. Roger, Richard, Edward. They all signed her dance card for a chance to waltz with the most beautiful girl in the sweeping, blush rose dress. It would be her demise.

Alexander claimed her early, convinced the other boys to back off, as only he could. The evening was warm, perfect to tease all male admirers in the ravishing off-the-shoulder dress. Alexander's eyes glittered with desire, and he persuaded her to step outside to the courtyard and cool off. They settled at the back garden, away from the other couples stealing kisses in the dark of night.

At first, his kiss was sweet and eager, but soon, his lips bruised hers, harsh, almost angry. She begged him to stop, but he turned into a mad dog. He ripped the bodice of the beautiful dress, squeezed her breasts, and crushed the sounds of her screams with his mouth. The end came when he hiked her skirts up and took her, there, on the freshly turned flowerbed, under the sycamore tree. No one could see, no one could hear. She crumpled in a heap, alone, almost unconscious, tears streaming down dirty cheeks.

Sometime later, a voice called out, soft, questioning, "Miss Williams, are you all right? Did you fall? Can I help you?"

Through cracked lips, she called to the young man, "Get Sarah, my maid, quick." She lay on one side, her back to him, unwilling for him to see the destruction.

Within minutes, Sarah collapsed beside her, knees smashing the flowers in the manicured beds. "Please, Robert, help me get her home."

The memory disappeared at the shake of her head. The beauty was gone…the innocent girl vanished. Robert Squire kept her secret and did the proper thing, and in time, his core goodness, compassion, and strength melted the stone in her heart. Love found them, but Priscilla never entirely forgot Alexander Adams. "This will not do. It does no good to mull over the past. I cannot go back."

Chapter Fourteen

Morning dawned, a pearl gray, and rain was in the forecast. Robert Squire sighed. "We can't be bothered by rain. We have an appointment with Mrs. Kirby."

Ruth's room remained locked when Mr. Squire tried the knob and no sound came when he tried to convince his daughter to come out.

Sarah told them Ruth did open the door to accept the breakfast tray, but wouldn't talk. "Best leave her alone for a while. It's shock, distress. I will see to her." The maid curtseyed and walked quickly toward the kitchen.

"I am sure she is right, dear. We *should* leave her alone. It all has to sink in. Let's meet with Mrs. Kirby, and see if we can find a way out of this mess." Robert Squire felt empowered this morning. The dilemma plagued him all night, and finally, determined fate would have a hand in the outcome.

"Yes, we'll go see Mrs. Kirby and explain what happened. It can not be helped," Priscilla agreed.

They arrived at the country estate close to nine o'clock. Mrs. Kirby greeted them and ushered them in with an offer of tea. She looked haggard, tired, as if she had not slept.

"Mrs. Kirby...Elizabeth, pardon me for saying this, but you look rather frazzled. I hope it is not on our account. Did you not sleep well?" Mrs. Squire asked.

"Actually, a situation has come to light, and I am at a loss as to how to handle it. I am curious about your urgent visit. Is Ruth all right? You sounded rather upset on the telephone last night." The cup rattled in her hand, and a stray wisp of hair slipped out of it's confinement.

Mrs. Squire shifted in her chair. "We have also become aware of an unpleasant state of affairs which is going to affect the engagement of Peter and Ruth. I am afraid we will have to call it off. It's quite out of our control, and we hope you will find it in your heart to understand. We are all quite beside ourselves with grief over this."

Elizabeth looked from one to the other. "Did you say call off the engagement?"

"Well…I am afraid…I can explain, of course. We hoped we could keep it private. Of course, if it will help you understand…" Mrs. Squire explained.

Elizabeth sat up straight. "No, no. I mean, I would like to know, certainly, but actually…I, well…my problem will also affect the engagement. Peter has not returned home since last night. His wagon is in the barn and the horses not fed. I am very worried."

Ruth's mother reached out a hand and placed it over Elizabeth's. "What is wrong? What happened?"

"We had a visitor yesterday, a woman from the old country. She recently lost her parents and has no family left. Twenty-seven years ago, a contract was signed between our two families. This woman and Peter are … well … betrothed. Since birth. The contract was in her pocketbook, and threats issued if we did not honor it. She would take it to the courts. When I told Peter about it, he went wild with anger. He wants Ruth, says they have talked and find each other mutually attractive and compatible. He wants your daughter and no other. I couldn't get him to even consider meeting this woman. When she came back last night to talk, of course, he wasn't here. I had a devil of a time getting her to settle down. After a half hour of threats and innuendos, I finally persuaded her to leave. I am beside myself with worry."

The Squires exchanged glances. "We have not seen Ruthie since last evening. I assumed she was in her room, according to our maid. You do not suppose they might be together?" Mrs. Squire said.

"Does Ruth know about your dilemma? Have you talked to her about it? Would you mind sharing it with me?"

Mrs. Squire looked at Robert. He nodded his assent.

"Well, you see, we've fallen on hard times. A second mortgage on our home is in default. Robert's articles are not selling as well as before. The banker called us in and gave us a choice. If we give our daughter's hand in marriage to him, he will wipe the slate clean. We can save our home. At first, I thought it a good arrangement, but now…I don't know. It would be a step up in society, a nice home in a good district, and she would be envied by all her friends. Should I make my daughter suffer for my mistakes, my transgressions? Now, you tell me of their mutual love for each other. What am I to make of it? Oh my, how have we gotten ourselves into this mess? We only wanted the best for our children. Do you think they ran off together, Elizabeth?"

"I don't know. It is not like Peter to neglect his duties or the business. I expect I will begin receiving calls from irate customers when they do not find their morning milk. On top of all the rest, I am afraid I cannot handle much more. What should we do?'

"Let them be, I say," Robert spoke for the first time.

"Let them be? How, Robert? We will have Eric Horton breathing down our necks with a foreclosure summons, maybe worse—and what of Elizabeth, facing charges by this woman? We cannot just let it be."

The room was quiet, the clock on the small mantle sounded the hour. No one gave an answer.

Robert broke the silence, "Time to go, dear. We need to face Mr. Horton, tell him what we decided. It is the right thing to do, after all."

"Yes, you are right. It may be too late anyway, if the children ran off. Of course, Ruth is still only seventeen, but if they go away and wait until her eighteenth birthday, nothing can be done. We may as well begin to look for an apartment in the city. Mrs. Kirby, I do not know how to help you with the problem you have right now. We are always available if you need to talk. I hope this does not affect our friendship, for we think very highly of you and your family."

Elizabeth rose unsteadily. It was evident she was tired. The warm glow, usually on her cheeks, was nowhere to be found. Robert thought she looked pale and fragile.

"Thank you so much for coming. I appreciate your concern and your frankness. I think I agree with you, Mr. Squire. Let them be. We must deal with the wreckage ourselves. The children did not create these problems. Please, promise me if you find them, let me know. Tell Peter, it is all right. I understand, and I love him. I will do the same for you."

The porch was crowded as the three said their good byes, but their voices stilled at the arrival of a black taxicab from the city.

Chapter Fifteen

"No, Ruth, you don't understand," Sarah began.

"I think I do. Please don't patronize me. Mother's life has been a lie and Father her victim."

Peter reached out. "Ruth, you mustn't judge your mother until you know all the facts. Does she know about the information you came across? Give her a chance to explain her side."

Sarah went to the vanity and opened the bottom drawer. "Look, Ruth. I haven't shown these to you, more letters. Aye, your mother was young, and maybe vain and spoiled, but an incident at the dance changed her forever. Your father knew and married her just the same. I was instructed to destroy the dresses, the jewelry, and all the letters, but I couldn't. I found this hidden closet years ago and decided to hide everything in here. I don't know why I did it. Maybe to preserve the carefree girl she was before the worst night of her life destroyed all innocence."

"What are you talking about? She loved Alexander. Father was second choice. I don't want to read any more of her lies. So, please tell me why Mother and Alexander never married?"

"Wait here, Ruth." Sarah went to a shelf beside the vanity and pulled a package down from the top shelf. "You need to see this, so you will understand."

Ruth took the package of butcher paper and twine from Sarah's outstretched hands and looked into the maid's eyes. "What is it?"

"Open it."

Ruth sat on the vanity chair, placed the package in her lap, and gingerly untied the knotted string until it fell away from the paper. She carefully unfolded the brittle tissue and beautiful ruffles of rose material burst forth. "Is it a dress, the one she wore that night?"

"Aye, but unfold it and look closely."

Peter helped pull the dress out of its confines and laid it across the vanity table.

Ruth gasped at the site. The bodice was torn almost to the waistline, and mud smeared across the skirt front and back. "Sarah, what is this? Why is it damaged so badly?"

In one word, the story was told. "Alexander."

Ruth looked at Peter. He put an arm around her. "Are you saying Alexander…he tried to…?"

"Aye, little one. Your mother was assaulted—spoiled."

Silence permeated the room, and Ruth tried to make sense of Sarah's revelation. Finally, words croaked between clenched teeth. "But why? How? Sarah, what of her parents, how did he get away with it? I read the other letters. He was a captain in the Navy. I'm sorry, but I don't believe you."

Sarah sat down beside the dress and slowly folded it back. "Her parents never knew. I found her in the garden, or rather your father did. She begged us not to tell anyone, not even her parents. You see, if it got out, no one would marry her…damaged goods. I helped her back to the house, cleaned her up, and put her to bed. Mr. and Mrs. Williams would have missed her, so I hurried back to the dance, and told them of a sudden illness, and I'd helped her back to the house.

They left the party immediately. Upon their arrival, Priscilla pretended to be asleep. The next day, orders were given for her to stay in bed, assuming it was something she ate, bad caviar, or something. I remember Mrs. Williams confronted the hostess, and the subject of food poisoning came up. Their relationship suffered irreparable damage."

Ruth shook her head. "What of the dress, didn't they wonder what happened to it? How could they just accept an excuse like that? From the sound of it, my mother lived for parties."

Sarah laughed. "Ruthie, you've seen all the dresses in the closet. There were so many; her parents never missed it. It was never an issue."

"How could you let Alexander off the hook? He should have been punished…exposed. I don't understand." Ruth took the gown from Sarah and studied it again. "He must have brutalized her by the look of the damage, and the mud. Did he…succeed?" She looked up at Sarah.

"Yes, dear. He forced himself on her."

Peter grabbed the dress and handed it back to Sarah. "Ladies, I know this is an unpleasant memory, and all these issues are hard to take. This happened almost twenty years ago, before Ruth was born. May I remind you of the present dilemma? My God, Ruth, they want to marry you off to Eric Horton, and I have a dire situation myself. It's why I'm here! We must address the present day and find a way to end our parent's interference."

"Peter is right, Ruth. We cannot stay in this closet forever. Time enough to figure out the past, it is the present needs to be addressed now," Sarah replied.

Ruth put a hand on Peter's arm. "I'm sorry. I got so wrapped up in Mother's drama, I completely forgot about our situation. Tell me, what has happened?"

"Please sit down, Ruth. You won't believe what I have to tell you."

Chapter Sixteen

Eric Horton slammed the ledger shut and rained a fist down on the cover with a thud. "I will not be mocked. It is clear they will not honor their promise. A full hour has past, plenty of time, and they have chosen not to show. Do they think they can do this to me?"

He gathered both coat and case, and marched out of the bank, purpose in his step.

The car sped through the city streets and came to a stop in front of the Squires' modest home. A cab sped away as he arrived, but he paid no attention to the occupants.

The pounding of his fist on the door echoed on the street. Eric was furious and wanted satisfaction. Frustrated there was no answer, he ran his fingers through his greasy hair and stormed down the steps to the car. He would take care of this matter his own way.

Eric stared at the back of his driver's shaved head, the chauffeurs' cap straight as an arrow. "Take me down to The Blue Feather Salon."

Uncharacteristically, the stout driver glanced quickly over one shoulder. "Did I hear you right, sir? The Blue Feather?"

"Keep your eyes on the road, and yes, that is what I said, now hurry."

They sped past the middle class part of town, and soon, the buildings took on a look of ill repair. Eric Horton tried to hide his nervousness as they went deeper into the shady district. He had only been down here once before. A shudder ran through him at the memory.

Women didn't flock around him, even as a young man. From mediocre stock, awareness found him early. The females in this town wanted money. Even though he achieved a modicum of success in the banking business, women avoided him. After a particularly lonely night at home drinking port, he decided to do something about it.

Eric summoned his driver, Audie, and asked where to find female company for the night. The Blue Feather became his destination. The trouble began when he told Audie not to wait; he would catch a taxi home.

Inside the smoke-filled speakeasy, women were plentiful. Decked out in their short, fringed dresses, colorful feathers standing at attention from their sequined headbands, they all but smothered Eric with attention. One in particular who called herself Emma Lou singled him out, plied him with drink, and emptied his pockets of every last dime. He had no money for either a taxi or to call from the pay phone for his driver. The worst part—he never even got upstairs with her ... all his money had vanished. He remembered the man who rescued him to a tee. Eric was digging through his pockets when someone sat down beside him.

"You busted, buddy?" the man in the black pinstriped suit asked.

Eric wobbled on the barstool. "I'm afraid I am. Don't know what happened. Had plenty of money when I came in, guess I drank too much."

"I'll be glad to help you out. Need money for a cab?" The stranger slapped Eric on the back.

"I'd be obliged. I'll pay you when I get home," Eric slurred.

"No need. Here's my card. I like you. You're my kind of people. This one is on me, and if you ever need anything, I'm the one to call."

Eric couldn't help but notice the black shirt, the white tie, and the matching trilby hat on his head. "Oh no, I insist. I want to pay you back as soon as I arrive home. I wouldn't want to be indebted."

"Maybe you didn't hear me right, my man. It's on me. Get my meaning? Of course, I might need a favor one day, *capisce?*" The man draped an arm around Eric's shoulder.

Eric's mind sobered at the heaviness of the man's appendage. "Sure, of course. I'm a banker in the city. If there is anything I can ever do for you…"

"The name's Giovanni Zapelli, or 'Johnny the Nose,' and I know exactly who you are, where you work, and more importantly, where you live." The Nose withdrew his arm, clapped Eric on the back, and motioned for a giant sized hulk in the corner. "My, uh, employee here will drive you home. See ya around, Horton."

Eric called after the Nose, "Uh, thank you Mr. Zapelli, er…Johnny."

A tip of his Mafioso hat, and the Nose disappeared through a back door.

The ride home was uneventful, but Eric felt great unease as the behemoth driver delivered him straight to his door without any directions. He swore never to venture out like that again and was glad his own chauffer didn't witness the stupid event.

Eric became increasingly apprehensive after the unfortunate encounter, though. Every few weeks, an unsavory, thug-like man dressed in a pinstriped suit would appear at his bank, walk around the foyer, nod in Eric's direction, and leave. He knew the other shoe would drop some day. Little did he know *he* would be the one to initiate a second encounter.

Here he was, speeding toward The Blue Feather again, deciding to strike first, and maybe get the monkey off his back.

The car stopped in front of the speakeasy, and this time he asked Audie to wait. Sober and sure of himself, he walked through the door of The Blue Feather in search of the Nose.

◆◆◆◆

Elizabeth's hand flew to her mouth. "Oh, no. It's her."

Priscilla touched the other woman's shoulder. "Would you like us to stay, Elizabeth?"

"Yes, yes, I would. Could you? I don't know if I can talk to her by myself. She is very determined. How I wish I knew where to find Peter."

Hattie Morgenstern approached the porch. "Mrs. Kirby. I am making one more attempt to make contact with your son. You cannot keep him from me forever. I will not leave until I speak to him."

"Miss Morgenstern, please, won't you come in? This is Mr. and Mrs. Squire. They are Peter's fiancée's parents. They were leaving, but have agreed to stay. Perhaps we can all come to some sort of understanding."

Hattie Morgenstern shook her head. "I have no need to talk to these people. They are the imposters. I am the one with the right to call Peter fiancée." She swept past the Squires and into the house.

The three others exchanged glances, but said nothing. The Squires followed Mrs. Kirby into the house.

Hattie took the high back chair; chin high, hands folded.

"I will get some fresh tea." Elizabeth turned to her other guests. "Please seat yourselves." She returned, tray in hand.

The Squires sat on the settee. Mrs. Squire attempted conversation with the young woman. "I understand you are from the old country. You must be very excited to be here in the United States. Is this your first trip here?"

Hattie turned a cold stare to the older woman. "It is none of your business why I am here. We have nothing to say to each other. You have stolen my fiancée."

"We have stolen nothing, Miss Morgenstern. We came here to cancel the engagement. But…Peter and Ruth are missing. I am afraid there is nothing we can do now. If they have decided to be together, we are powerless to stop them."

For the first time, Hattie's face looked full of doubt, unguarded. "Run off?" she asked. "What do you mean?"

"I mean, we cannot find either one of them," Mrs. Squire answered.

Elizabeth set the tea tray on the side table. "That's right, Hattie. We were discussing what to do."

The screen door banged shut, and a collective gasp filled the room.

"No one has run off. We are both right here." Peter stood in the doorway, Ruth by his side.

◆◆◆◆

Johnny the Nose looked amused at Horton's fumbled request. Eric's palms began to sweat. *Did I just ask the Nose to take out Peter Kirby? Will he laugh or just shoot me?* He rocked from side to side, first one foot, then the other.

"A broad, Horton? You want me to take this Kirby guy out for a broad? I don't know, not exactly my style. I got bigger fish to fry. I operate in the big time, ya know. How much money you got?" The cigar in his mouth bobbed up and down; he pulled it out and rolled it between his index finger and thumb.

Eric reached into the inside jacket pocket and brought out a thick envelope full of hundred dollar bills. "I know it's not much, but I can get more. Think of it as a down payment."

Johnny snatched the envelope, opened it, checked the contents, and stuffed it in his holster. "I'll sleep on it, banker. I'll let you know. Now get out of here before I plug ya."

The same hulk of a man that drove Eric home on that previous encounter clapped a hand on his shoulder and pushed him to the door. Horton tried to glance behind him as he moved forward, but the Nose *and* his money were gone.

◆◆◆◆

Eric paced the study floor until he thought a path might appear in the expensive carpet. Finally, tired of waiting, he decided to go back to the office. Enraged at the turn of events, he made a quick decision to foreclose on the Squires. "This was nonsense. I should never have trusted their word. Now, they will suffer the consequences."

The document did not take long to prepare. A final swirl at the end of his signature, and he lifted the telephone and called the sheriff's office for a deputy to make the delivery. After the officer left, he leaned back in the office chair and clasped both hands behind his head. "I wish I could see their faces when they receive the summons."

"Mr. Horton, how is it your work is so complete you have time to daydream on my time?" Eric sat up so fast, his feet tangled in the chair. The boss's face was red, and the anger in his voice struck fear in Eric's heart. "What is it you are so gleeful about?" his superior demanded.

"Why, I was not exactly gleeful, sir. A foreclosure was issued on a client…one who has been delinquent for a very long time. I am simply satisfied with the fact no stone was left unturned to save the account." Eric did not get along with the elder bank officer…an ancient, white-haired stick in the mud. He needed to retire and let Eric step into those shoes. The old goat did not show signs of giving up the position, however.

"We never take pleasure in a client's hard time, Mr. Horton. I trust you completed each step, given them every chance. Be sure I will follow up on your handling of this account." The door slammed as he left.

Eric quit nodding after the door banged shut and slumped in his seat. Now, what was he to do? If the boss looked too closely, he might find the discrepancy. *Maybe there is time to intercept the courier.*

◆◆◆◆

Deafening silence permeated the room. No one spoke until Peter took the lead. "We came to declare our desire to wed. I know about the foreclosure and the attempt to marry Ruth off to Eric Horton. That marriage will not happen." He pointed to the young female stranger. "You must be the woman from my homeland. Too bad you came all this way for nothing because I will not marry you or any other. It is Ruth I want." Peter shifted his attention to the Squires. "I have the ability to loan the money for your mortgage arrears. Please—do not waste breath by trying to refuse. I paid good attention to my business, and since Ruth will be my wife, my duty is to help her parents. That is all I have to say. It is final." He put one arm around Ruth as if afraid she would flee.

Again, no one spoke. Hattie stood slowly to face Peter, chin high. "You forget, I have a contract and will take it to court, Peter. All I ask is for a few moments alone to discuss this matter. As I understand it, the engagement between you and this girl is arranged. It is no different from what I propose. Surely, you can give me the same consideration you did this poor mite of a girl."

Peter looked at his mother, and saw pleading in her eyes, and a nod of agreement. He let out a loud sigh, slumped his shoulders, and turned toward the door. "We will be in the garden." He offered an arm, and the two disappeared into the cool winter air.

Ruth stood in absolute silence through it all. She looked at her parents…to Mrs. Kirby, and back to her parents. "Why are you here, Mother?"

Priscilla Squire hung her head. "We came to cancel the engagement. Ruth, our senses are restored. You cannot believe we wanted…*I* really wanted you to marry the awful Mr. Horton. Peter is the one you should marry. Worry of losing the home you were born in twisted my common sense. Of course, you will marry Peter—if we can get him out of this mess. Will you forgive me, daughter? I fear I've been misguided for quite a while now."

Ruth made quick strides to sit between her parents. "Oh Mother, Father. Of course, I forgive you. At first, to marry a man I did not know appeared absurd. Now, I have gotten to know him, and it is what I want."

"What of this new woman, Ruth? What of her?" Robert Squire asked.

"Peter will handle it, Father. I know he will find a solution." One hand covered his.

An eternity passed, almost an hour.

Ruth paced the room, glancing at the door, and back at her parents. *Why is it taking so long? Surely, he can convince her to drop this nonsense.*

Conversation ceased and everyone sipped tea, china cups rattling the only sound in the room.

Peter and Hattie returned. The unwelcome woman hung on Peter's arm and gazed at him as if he were Prince Charming. Peter cleared his throat. "We have an announcement to make."

◆◆◆◆

The garden enclosure was cold, damp, and smelled of mold. "Like my life." Ruth kicked at a loose stone on the pathway. Alone on the cold hard bench, the world looked dark, indeed. He betrayed her and chose the snooty Ms. Morgenstern. *How can it be? Well, fine. I don't want to get married anyway, right? I fought against it. Freedom is what I'm after. My parents might lose their house. As for me? Off to boarding school. I will not stay here with Peter and his new bride. I'm too young to marry, anyway. A fresh start, a change of scenery is what I need.* Tears erupted and streamed down her face.

A spider crawled across the bench, a harmless garden variety. "Where are you off to spider? Off to weave your web of deceit?" The eight-legged arachnid disappeared into the greenery. *Hattie Morgenstern – almost ten years older. She must know all the tricks to seduce a man. I am but a girl, with no experience. I cannot hope to compete with a woman of the world. Of course, he would want her over me. I am proud of Mother, though. For the first time, I saw true concern as Peter was about to make the announcement. She grabbed my arm and dragged me out of the house, Father close behind. At least, I didn't have to suffer the humiliation of hearing Peter's treachery.*

A light rain dusted the greenery, and she hugged herself for warmth, wishing it were Peter's arms around her. *I know I should go in. There is a lot to do to get ready to leave in the morning.* A trickle of tears drizzled down her cheeks, again. *Why should I care? I have my freedom, more or less. Boarding school won't be so bad. I'll meet new friends and be away from my parents. We need space between us, and our relationship needs to heal.* She sneezed.

"Ruth, you should not be out here. You'll catch your death of cold." Father wrapped a cloak around her shivering shoulders.

"It won't matter, Father. My life is over anyway." An involuntary sob escaped.

Robert Squire sat beside her on the cold bench. "You may think so now, Ruthie. The school will broaden your horizons, and eventually, you will find what it is you want to do with your life."

"Father, why did Mother go to the extremes she did? First with Peter, then horrible Eric Horton. Does she dislike me so very much?" Ruth rested her head on his damp shoulder.

He craned his neck to look at her. "Dislike you? Mother loves you very deeply."

She sat up straight. "How can she—to sell me off to the highest bidder like that?"

"Princess, you do not understand. Mother sees me as a failure. I am a mere writer, and she aspired to much higher achievements. Oh, her love was true in the beginning. It was very mysterious being married to a writer. Her friends were all very envious. Unfortunately, my writing kept me locked in the study for much of the time. The excitement wore off."

Ruth thought of the ball gowns and jewelry in the closet…the letters, and was about to ask him about all of it when Mother shouted from the doorway.

"You two get inside this instant. It's raining, and Ruth needs her rest."

The spell was broken, and the time with Father was over. He squeezed her hand. They went arm in arm into the house as Priscilla held the door open.

Ruth still found it difficult to look at her mother. There were so many questions. She could not bring herself to sit down and talk. For a moment, Ruth thought Mother might take this opportunity to have a heart-to-heart discussion. They both hesitated outside Ruth's bedroom door, but Mrs. Squire walked away with a brief good night, and Ruth was left alone, once again. She made sure her parents descended the stairs, waited a moment, and crept down the hall. Time to take a chance.

Chapter Seventeen

Sarah watched as Ruth ran to the door of Mrs. Squire's room, and knew she should stop the girl, keep the truth from her, but she had interfered enough. Instead, she turned away and disappeared into the shadows.

◆◆◆◆

Ruth glanced back to see if the way was clear and entered the forbidden sanctuary. The glass doorknob sparkled like before, and she grasped and turned the handle. The drab gray dresses hung as if in defiance. *Would I ever resort to wearing such unbecoming attire?* She followed the wall of the closet until it turned the corner. "Oh, no, it cannot be. Where is everything? Where did it all go?" Empty hangers chaperoned the forsaken, bare shelves. All the colorful gowns...gone, no matching shoes or jewelry illuminated the dark wardrobe. The white vanity sat alone. She rushed forward and pulled open drawers—empty. "Mother's letters are gone. I put them right back here, in this drawer. I need to read the rest of them, find out what happened between her and Captain Adams. I need answers." Scalding tears burned her eyes. "Peter, oh, Peter. Why did you desert me and choose Hattie? Who is to guide me?"

A slight rustle startled her. She looked up. "Sarah. How did you know I was here?"

"I'm the only one who knew about this false closet until you found it. We need to talk." Sarah entered slowly, kneeled beside Ruth, and laid a hand on her back. "You are confused, my dear. I saw you slip in here. I promised myself I wouldn't interfere again, but you cannot handle all this alone."

Ruth sat up and wiped the tears away. "Yes, Sarah, I wanted to read the rest of the letters, find out how Mother made the decision to marry Father. My heart is broken. So much has changed in only a week. The little escapade of mine, sneaking out with Ginny…so childish of me. I was angry with Mother. I thought it impossible she would want me to marry a perfect stranger. But now, Sarah, I have lost him. He is going to marry the other woman, and I am desolate. Can you fall in love so quickly, or is it only a girl's foolishness?" she sobbed.

"Why do you say Peter is going to marry the other woman, Ruth? Did ya hear him say it? Did ya stay and hear him out or run away like a little child?"

"Of course, I ran out. They went outside and talked…forever. When they returned, their arms were entwined, and he said they had an announcement to make. What else was I to think? They are going to marry. He is going to honor the contract to save his mother. He is an honorable man, and I have lost him."

Sarah took Ruth's hand and pulled her to her feet. "Come with me, Ruth. I have something to show you."

She jerked her hand back. "Leave me alone, Sarah, enough of your mysteries. My mind is made up. I am going to boarding school. We went directly to the telegraph office and bought my train ticket."

The maid grabbed her hand, again, and pulled harder. "No, Ruthie, you are coming downstairs with

me. Ye must see this." She practically dragged Ruth out of the bedroom and into the hallway.
"Oh, all right. Stop pulling. What is it you want me to see?"
"Just come. All will be clear in a moment, but be quiet."
They tiptoed down the stairs and stood in front of the parlor.
"Okay, Sarah what am I supposed to see?"
The maid pressed a finger to her lips. "Quiet." Sarah opened the door a crack and guided her to peek through the slim opening.
Ruth stooped over and tried to see inside.
Mother and Father sat on the settee, snuggled close.
Ruth stood up and whispered, "It is Mother and Father, so what?"
Sarah pushed her back to the door. "Watch."
Her eye pressed to the opening, Ruth focused again, and saw something she never before had witnessed. Their heads were nestled together, Father's hand lifted Mother's chin, and he kissed her, gently. Priscilla Squire blushed like a young bride and rubbed her nose, flirtatiously, with Roberts.
Ruth could not take her eyes from the intimate scene. It was shocking, but pleasant, at the same time. Mother's face softened, the stern, pursed look disappeared, and a pink color bloomed on her cheeks. Father lifted his hand and pulled the pin out of Mother's hair. It fell over her shoulders and immediately, the transformation gave Ruth a glimpse of her mother as a young girl.

She had never seen Mother's hair down, and all of a sudden, Ruth recognized the girl she saw in the closet. "Sarah, what has happened to my parents?"

"They have found one another again, Ruthie. Their love for you forged the path back to the love that bound them, so many years ago. Come, we must go. They don't need to catch us spying on them." She pulled Ruth away.

Back in Ruth's room, Sarah explained, "You see, things are not always as they appear."

"But why now? I am going away to boarding school. Are they glad to be rid of me?"

"Oh, Ruth, you are a silly girl. Of course, they don't want to be rid of you. Your mother doubted her decision after years of struggle with your father. You imagined her in the guest room as a girl. She wanted jewels, parties, society, and popularity. Those things did not happen with your father. He was a writer, and being a writer is a lonely profession. Not all the fault lies with him. After you were born, Ms. Squire focused all the attention on you because of loneliness. So, your father retreated farther into his study. There was no room for him, anymore. You were her world and she transferred every hope and expectation on you."

Ruth stood, went into the hallway, and gazed down the stairs. "I am a disappointment. Her dreams were not my dreams. It was a vicious circle, wasn't it?"

"In a way, dearie. It's the human condition, after all. I made you aware of this because I do not want you to run off with out fighting for what you want. You want Peter, don't you?"

"I think I want Peter, but with what has happened, maybe I don't know my own mind. Is it love or attraction?"

A clatter in the street shifted their attention. Sarah reached the window first. "Oh my, it is the sheriff's car and awful Mr. Horton. What could they be wantin' now?

"They cannot be foreclosing, can they? Oh, my goodness, do you think he is here to ask for my hand in marriage again? We must hide, Sarah. I can't look at him. I certainly don't want to meet him face to face. Please, Sarah, hide me." Ruth turned and grabbed Sarah's arms. "Please."

"Come with me, quickly." Sarah hurried out of the bedroom door.

They ran down the hall and back into her mother's room.

"Back into the closet?"

Sarah shoved her inside. "It's a safe hiding place."

They fought through the drab dresses, turned the corner, and huddled together waiting to hear the dreaded summons to meet Mr. Horton. It never came. An hour passed, and Ruth worried Sarah's job might be in jeopardy if she didn't show herself soon. They decided to sneak through the guest room and down the hall to Ruth's bedroom. They ran to the window to see if Horton's car was still there.

"Sarah, he's gone. Mother didn't call for me. What do you suppose it means?"

"I'm not sure. I better scoot back to the kitchen. If I find out anything, I'll come tell ya. You stay locked in your room." Sarah hurried out the door.

Ten minutes later, Mother called to Ruth from the hallway. "Ruthie, dear. Dinner is served in about ten minutes, and your father and I want to dine all together. Please come down."

Ruth called back. "Certainly, Mother. I'll be right there." She went to the window again, just to make sure Eric Horton's car had not returned. "I don't want to walk into a trap." Dressed in a sky blue dinner dress, she joined them in the dining room.

Conversation remained light. The banker's name never came up, and no one talked about Peter. Ruth, fascinated, watched her parent's newfound affection. They couldn't take their eyes off each other. Every time a dish was passed around the table, their hands touched and lingered. Ruth wanted to talk about that night so long ago—Alexander, the dress, but, the mood was sweet and loving, and she didn't want to break the spell. *Maybe I will never know, and Mother may never agree to share the details, but some way, somehow, I will find the truth.*

Chapter Eighteen

Peter did not anticipate the stampede of Priscilla and Robert Squire as he and Hattie re-entered the parlor. The announcement died in his throat when Mrs. Squire, with Ruth in tow, barreled past Peter, and out the door. In their haste, they knocked Peter into the obviously unsuspecting Miss Morgenstern, who crashed to the floor. Her scream of pain stopped Peter from pursuing the fleeing Squires.

"My ankle, I've twisted my ankle." Hattie writhed in obvious pain.

Peter watched, helplessly, as Ruth raced away in the automobile. His duty, at the moment, was to see to the injury of their guest.

Elizabeth and Peter carried the stricken woman to the sofa. While Elizabeth ran to get an ice pack, Peter tried to calm her. "Try not to exert yourself, Hattie. The ice pack will help, and if the swelling is too much, we will take you into town to see Doc Atwood. He fixes all the broken bones and mishaps of this family."

"Why in heaven's name did they run out of here so fast? Oh, I think I've bruised my shoulder, too." Hattie grabbed the offending appendage and winced.

"Mother, where is that ice pack?" Peter shouted.

Elizabeth rushed in. "Here, son. Here it is."

Peter applied the remedy to the ankle in question. "I don't understand why they left. They didn't give me a chance to explain. What can they be thinking?"

Hattie moaned at the touch of the cold compress.

"There there, dear. The ice will dull the pain in a moment. Try to hold steady," Elizabeth crooned.

Peter stood and grabbed his overcoat. "I must go after them, Mother. They misunderstood. I have to explain."

"You will do no such thing, Peter. I cannot tend to Hattie alone. Her ankle might be broken, for all we know. If that is the case, we must carry her to the doctor. I can't do it alone. There will be time for explanations, Peter. Right now, Hattie is hurt. Your place is here." Elizabeth adjusted the ice pack and patted Hattie's free hand.

"You are right, as always, Mother. I'm sorry Hattie. We'll see you are right as rain, first." Peter hung his coat on the hook and returned to sofa. "How is it feeling? Better?"

"I can't tell. The ice has dulled the pain some. Is it swelling?" Hattie peeked under the makeshift bandage.

He moved the compress to the side. "It doesn't look swollen. Let's keep the ice on it, though. How is your shoulder? Do we need to ice it, as well?"

Hattie moved her shoulder around, shook her head. "No, I just grazed it against the door jamb. I think it will be fine."

Elizabeth sighed and took a seat across from Peter and Hattie. "What in the world was all the commotion? Can you think why they ran out like that, Peter?"

He shook his head. "My only thought is I used the wrong choice of words. I said I had an announcement. They must have determined I meant I would wed Hattie. An explanation is in order. I need to pay a visit this evening and explain. Poor Ruth, she must be beside herself. I can't let her think I've compromised the Squires' good name. The longer I let this go without explanation, the angrier they will become."

Hattie sat up straighter and touched the ankle gingerly. "You know, Peter, I'll be fine. It's not swelling. Why don't you go on ahead and explain to the Squires. Your mother and I will sit a bit longer…until the pain dies down.

"Mother?" Peter looked at Elizabeth.

"Only if you're sure, Hattie. I can't lift you by myself, you know."

"I'm fine. You go on, Peter." Hattie pointed toward the door.

He snatched a jacket from the hook and stopped to smile at the two women. "I'll return as soon as I can explain to the Squires. Thank you, Hattie. Tomorrow, if you can walk, we'll set up the meeting we talked about."

Peter bounded out the door and into the family automobile. The long road into town took an eternity. Panic became palatable as he realized what Ruth and her parents must have thought about the so-called announcement. A dog ran across the road, but he didn't even swerve. People honked and shook their fists, his speed out of control. Finally, he arrived at the Squire's house, threw the gear in park, and raced to the front door.

After a frantic banging of the brass knocker, Peter realized no one was home. "Where could they have gone?" He fished around in his pocket, found a scrap of paper and a pencil, and scribbled a note. *Please, I need to talk to all of you. There has been a misunderstanding. I am not going to marry Miss Morgenstern. I want to marry Ruth, if she will have me. Call me at your earliest convenience. Peter.*

He slipped the note in the crack of the door, looked up to Ruth's bedroom window, and when he didn't see any movement, reluctantly walked back to his car. "Maybe I should wait. They could return any minute." He shook his head. "No, I can't leave Mother with Hattie for long. What if the ankle got worse? I'll have to wait until morning."

He sped back home, hoping beyond hope, they had called, and all was well.

Hattie Morgenstern stood at the window in the front parlor. "Did you talk to them, Peter? Is everything straightened out?"

He removed his coat and returned it to the hook. "No one answered the door. I can't imagine where they went. No one called here?" Peter looked around for his mother.

"No one. The good news is my leg feels better. I don't think it is hurt as bad as we thought. See? I'm able to stand on it, now." Hattie took a step toward Peter.

"Be careful, you might not feel the worst of it until tomorrow. I don't think you should be standing. Come…sit down. Where's Mother?" He led her to the sofa.

She arranged the full skirt around slim ankles and smiled at Peter. "In the kitchen, making a snack for the boys upon their return from school. I assured her I was fine."

Peter bowed toward Hattie. "Please, excuse me. I'd like to have a word."

He found her in the kitchen hovered over a turkey sandwich. "Mother, what is wrong? You're crying."

Elizabeth flung herself into Peter's arms. "Oh Son, I've made such a mess of things. I meddled in your life, and now look. So many people hurt. All I wanted was to find a way to make you happy. Poor Ruth, and her parents must be furious with me, and Hattie…she came so far to honor a stupid contract. Her ankle is probably broken. What will happen to her? Will you ever forgive me?"

He pushed away and looked down at her wet face. "Mother, stop crying. Of course, I forgive you. Hattie's ankle is fine. No one let me finish my announcement. Didn't Hattie tell you what I was about to say?"

"Hattie, tell me? Tell me what, Son?"

"Sit down, Mother. I have the most amazing story to tell you."

Chapter Nineteen

Ruth was glad they drove directly from Peter's house to the ticket office. She barely listened at the discussion of how they must get her out of town, away from the scandal. Boarding school became the focus now—salvage what they could of Ruth's reputation. Mother made it clear Ruth would not marry Eric Horton, either. She remained silent as her mother talked to the head mistress of the school. Nothing mattered, anymore.

The train rocked back and forth, as it chugged down the track, and lulled Ruth into a fitful sleep. The night before the departure for school, sleep eluded her. Dreams of Peter, and fear of a new life, had her staring at the ceiling. She felt betrayed and lost. The noisy train's brakes hissed steam, brought the iron horse to a stop, and jerked her awake. Someone was to meet and escort her to the school. *Maybe there will be a sign from the designee, something for me to recognize.* A tremor of fear shivered down her spine.

The train emptied slowly, and Ruth elected to hang back, scan the crowd, and have the first look at the person who was to give her a ride. At last, all the other passengers were off, and she was the last person in the car. Reluctant to exit the security of the train's shelter, she finally shook off the trepidation, squared her shoulders, and moved to the exit. People walked to-and-fro, greeting friends and family, and retrieving their baggage. A tentative step down the stairs, eyes cast downward so not to trip over her own feet, she landed on the platform. Only at the bottom did she dare look up, afraid to see what manner of person came to collect her.

Horror stories of boarding school filled her mind. The dull uniforms, the jailor-type head mistresses, and the strict rules and punishments for infractions of those rules. Freedom? All of a sudden, she was not too sure of the meaning of the word. Maybe she rushed into a more restricted atmosphere. What did it matter now? All was lost. The only good thing—she did not have to marry the awful Eric Horton.

How she argued to get Ginny to go to the school, too. She missed her friend. There would only be strangers here, and an ally would be nice to have. Ginny refused. She chose to stay in Detroit, although Ruth knew it was more about a certain boy. Ginny always had an eye for George Pollard. Her best friend remained in the city, and Ruth set out on a new adventure, solo.

Both hands clutched the brown leather purse in front of her, but she braved the fear long enough to raise her head, and scan the crowd. No one. The crowd thinned, and Ruth decided the school forgot to send anyone. A long wooden bench sat in front of the ticket office. She walked over and sat down. No choice left but to wait.

The crowd disbursed as everyone found their way to family and friends until Ruth was completely alone. Should she ask the ticket master where the school was and walk? She stood and went to the counter.

"Yes, miss? The next train will not be along for another hour."

"No, I was supposed to meet someone here. I mean, they were to pick me up. I am going to the boarding school, and well, no one is here. Can you tell me the way to the school?"

A tap on her shoulder made her jump. "Are you Ruth Squire?"

She turned to see a tall, dark haired man. "Oh yes, I am. Are you from the school?"

"Yes, I'm Taylor. Cal Taylor. The head mistress sent me. Where are your bags?"

She pointed behind him. "Over there, on the platform. They were too heavy for me to lift. I am Ruth by the way."

"I know you are, Miss Squire, you said so before," he replied.

She felt the blood rush to her face. "Oh, I am sorry. It's all the travel, I guess."

The handsome man turned abruptly to retrieve the bags, and she took a moment to survey the back of Cal Taylor. He sported a long, black wool overcoat, and a black, derby hat sat a bit crooked on his head. He walked with purpose, maybe a little impatient. He hoisted a bag in each hand and nodded at Ruth. "Let's go. My auto is over there."

She followed—a little guilty about her lack of assistance. Once settled in the motorcar, he entered the highway without a word.

Ruth stole a glance. He acted distracted, like an unwilling participant in this rendezvous. "I'm sorry I took you away from your duties, Mr. Taylor. I know this is quite unusual to start in the middle of the term," Ruth spoke softly.

"No problem, miss. This *is* part of my duties at the school. Don't let it bother you." He cut his eyes in her direction. She saw a fleeting smile and sparkly green eyes that crinkled at the corners. Was he amused? Did he think her a silly inexperienced country girl? It was hard to read him. Her cheeks warmed, and she wondered if it would be best served to cease further conversation.

Before she could think of any more to say, he spoke. "What brings you here, Miss Squire? Trouble at home, or failing grades at your high school? Too many girls are dropping out of school. It's a shame, really."

Startled, she looked directly at him. "I am a perfectly good student, Mr. Taylor. It surely had nothing to do with my grades." Reluctant to explain further, she stared straight ahead, and remained quiet.

They drove in silence for a time, and Ruth watched the scenery—the rain soaked trees and winter gray houses. Instead of heading for the town, he took a road away from the populated area. "The school is in the country, Mr. Taylor?" She dared a look at him.

"No, the school is closer to the city. I am taking you to my house." He kept his eyes on the road.

Fear engulfed her. *Is he kidnapping me? Is he really from the school? Did I let a perfect stranger pick me up? What should I do?* "Please, Mr. Taylor, stop the car and let me out. I will walk. My parents will worry if they do not get a phone call to let them know I arrived safely." Her voice quavered.

Cal Taylor looked at her and smiled. "I'm sorry, Miss Squire, I didn't mean to frighten you. I simply thought you might like a nice home cooked meal and a cup of Mother's famous hot chocolate before you entered the cold domain of the boarding school. She always feeds the girls a meal before their first encounter with the head mistress. I promise; I am not a kidnapper."

Ruth examined his face, saw the easy smile, and the twinkle in his eyes. Her relief was audible as she blew out a long breath. "I apologize, Mr. Taylor. I didn't know. This is my first experience with boarding school. Please forgive me."

He reached over and patted her hand. "It is I who should apologize. I do this all the time, to all the new girls. Mother gets very angry with me, but for the most part, my job is very serious, and it lends a little of the unconventional to the day. Please forgive me. I didn't mean to frighten you."

She cut another quick look at him. *What could his job be at the school? It's a school for girls. I didn't think about men being on the campus. He looks a little older than I.* "What is it you do at the school, Mr. Taylor?" she ventured.

"Please, call me Cal. I actually graduated from the men's school a few blocks from the women's. I volunteer at Barkley's. I'm the official driver and all around jack-of-all-trades. Whenever the women require something only a man can do, they call me," he said.

"I see. I shall probably see you around the school, then."

They arrived at a modest farmhouse. It needed a little paint, and the yard looked neglected. Weeds overtook the flowers, chickens wandered around, pecking, here and there, at the ground.

Ruth's unease returned at the sight of the simple home. *Has he told me the truth? Does he not care for his own mother's place?*

"The school keeps me so busy, and while I look for permanent employment, it is hard to keep up with the demands of the farm. Mother keeps the house spotless, but cannot do the yard work. That is left to me, and I'm not doing such a great job, as you can see."

Ruth smiled, a little more relieved.

The car came to a stop, and Cal came around to open the auto door. A young golden retriever bounded around the house as she stepped out of the car.

Cal intercepted the exuberant pup, knelt, and scruffed his ears. "Joey, you silly dog. Miss Squire does not want your muddy paws all over her nice dress. You need to settle down, old boy."

"He is beautiful, Cal. How old is he?"

"Not quite a year, yet. Still a pup and ill-trained, I fear."

"Cal! Is this the new young lady? Get that dog away and bring her to the house." A lovely, plump, white-haired woman called from the porch.

"Coming, Mother." Cal made a grab at the dog's collar, but he scampered out of reach.

The dog sniffed the hem of Ruth's skirt. Cal called him off in a gruff voice, and Joey loped away, barking at the chickens in the yard.

"Come on, Ruth. You need to meet my mother." He took her arm and led the way to the front porch. "Mother, may I present Ruth Squire, the newest addition to Barkley Women's School."

Ruth reached out a hand when she arrived at the top step. "Nice to meet you, Mrs. Taylor. I appreciate your hospitality."

"Glad to do it, Miss Squire. It's a bit of a tradition around here. Please come in and shed your coat." The older woman stood aside and allowed her guest to enter first.

Once inside, there was a shuffle of coats, and Mrs. Taylor led Ruth through the house. On a long, wooden dining table, a full course meal beckoned—ham, mashed potatoes, a huge vegetable salad, rolls, and corn on the cob.

Ruth stopped in the doorway. "Oh, Mrs. Taylor, this is too much. I surely did not expect such an elaborate spread."

"It's nothing, child. This is a working farm, nothing more than ordinary fare. Please sit down."

Cal pulled out the heavy, oak chair for Ruth, moved to assist his mother, and ended up at the head of the table. The white, lace tablecloth looked a little fancy for a meal at noon, but it was lovely. Cal was right. The house was spotless and not overcrowded with knick-knacks. There was the basic, wooden furniture with a few pots of greenery placed here and there for warmth. The wooden floors were clean and shiny. This was a practical, well-organized woman.

"Now, Ruth, tell us a bit about yourself. You are from Detroit, we know already. What brings you here to our school?" the older woman began.

Ruth glanced from Cal back to his mother. "There is not much to tell, Mrs. Taylor. I struggled to stay in the girl's high school in Detroit, but a set of unfortunate circumstances led me here. I am a good student hoping for a fresh start. My parents and I need some time apart, I'm afraid. I suppose I was a bit troublesome to them. I am only a semester from graduation. They insist I graduate, unlike so many girls of the city, nowadays. After school, I hope to return home and to a normal life at the end of the term. *If* they want me back."

Cal's mother reached for a ceramic teapot and poured a most aromatic cocoa.

"Mrs. Taylor, this smells delicious. What is in it? I cannot wait to taste it."

"Be careful Ruth, it's hot. Don't burn your tongue," Mrs. Taylor cautioned. "We would not want your first day at our school to be spent in the infirmary."

Ruth picked up the cup, held it to her lips, and blew. "What do you mean, Mrs. Taylor? You keep saying our school. Do you work there also? Like Cal?"

Mrs. Taylor chuckled. "Well yes, I guess you could say I work there. I'm the head mistress."

Ruth's almost dropped the cup. "The head mistress? My goodness, Cal why didn't you tell me? I'm so embarrassed."

"Don't fret, my dear. I suppose Cal had you afraid you were being kidnapped, also. I scold him about his antics, but to no avail. I'm not surprised he didn't tell you. This is my tradition, to welcome the girls alone in my home. I like to get a good feel of each one, let them meet me in my home setting. It makes the transition easier for them. How is the chocolate, dear?"

Ruth sipped the hot liquid. "It is heavenly, Mrs. Taylor. I must know your secret."

"I'm afraid I never give out my secret. All the girls ask for it. Only upon graduation will I reveal it, and only then to the girl with the highest scores." She passed the potatoes while Cal laid a generous portion of ham on her plate.

"Now let's eat. After lunch, Cal will take you to the dormitory and help you get your bags up the stairs. A hall mother will give you a set of instructions and settle you into the school's schedule and routine. I hope you enjoy it here, Ruth. It is a good school, and our girls come from a variety of backgrounds. Those who take advantage of what we offer usually return to their homes to begin the lives they aspired to while here. I hope it holds true for you, too."

The rest of the meal was full of small talk and laughter, but Ruth remembered another meal when the mention of a secret ingredient came up in conversation. The thought of the dinner Mrs. Kirby prepared for her and Ginny plagued her mind. She too, refused to give her the secret ingredient and explained only the woman Peter married would have it. Hattie Morgenstern will have it now, she guessed. Ruth would never prepare Peter's favorite meal. She shook herself and realized Mrs. Taylor had asked her a question.

"Brothers and sisters? Oh no, I am an only child. It is probably a good thing. I have been a handful for my parents." She attempted a laugh.

A silence fell, and all three continued with their meal—forks and knives scraping the china plates, the only noise in the room.

Ruth looked at her hostess. "Do you teach cooking in this school, Mrs. Taylor?"

"Why yes, Ruth, we do. Have you an interest in cooking? Your mother didn't teach you how?"

"No, we had a maid. Her name is Sarah. She taught me a few things, but it dawned on me I know nothing about preparing a meal. I would like to learn. Is it too late to enter the class?"

"Not at all, my dear. We will arrange it for you. If you are finished, Cal will take you on to the school. I will meet with you tomorrow, and we will discuss your schedule. I am very pleased to make your acquaintance, Ruth. I hope your experience with our school will be a good one."

They shook hands, Ruth thanked her for the meal, and Cal escorted her to the car. Mrs. Taylor stood on the porch and waved as they drove away.

On the way to the school, Cal was silent. As they neared the town, he finally spoke. "I guess you are mad at me for my little game."

"I was at first. It was a mean trick. However, I forgive you. Your mother is a lovely person, and it was good to meet her that way, instead of an old stuffy office."

Cal chuckled. "Works every time."

Chapter Twenty

The dorm room was small, and by the look of it a roommate was already installed. She only hoped they would be as nice as her best friend, Ginny. *I've never shared a room with anyone before, except for sleepovers.* "It should be interesting."

"What should be interesting?" a voice asked behind her.

Ruth jumped and faced the woman in the doorway. "I…I was wondering about my roommate. My name is Ruth Squire, and I'm new here."

"Well, hello, Ruth. I am Doris and the roommate in question." The girl gave a mock curtsey, ran across the room, and hugged her.

All Ruth saw were braids, brown eyes, and freckles showcased in a plaid uniform skirt, navy blazer, white socks, and saddle shoes. "Happy to meet you Doris. I hope we will be fast friends."

"Of course we will. Have you met Cal yet? Of course you did, he drove you?" Doris flopped down on the empty bunk. "This is your bed. All your things will go over here in the armoire. See? We both have one." She opened the door of the empty, wooden closet. "My last roommate left weeks ago. Couldn't hack the all girl thing. I'm so glad to have a new one. Isn't Cal dreamy? All the girls have a crush on him."

Ruth laughed. "Slow down, Doris. I just got here, and don't know what to think of Cal. I just met him. There are more important things to think about now, and boys are not included."

"Oh pooh, don't be so serious. You won't make many friends being so stuffy."

"I see. Well, I promise to give your advice some thought. Right now, I need to get settled, unpack, and find the hall mother to go over my schedule." Ruth glanced around the sparsely furnished room, the only color a dark green spread and curtains.

"Follow me, I'll show you." Doris sprinted through the door, and Ruth had no choice but to trot after her.

After the class schedule was settled, Doris led her to the cafeteria where all the other girls gathered for their evening meal. She met all sorts of new friends, and retreated to the dorm room confused, excited, and melancholy. Sleep would elude her tonight, for sure—too many thoughts, too many distractions…her parents, the new school, and Peter. She lay in the narrow bunk praying for sleep, but continued to stare at the dull-white ceiling.

"Who are you thinking about, Ruth? I can tell you have something on your mind. Come on, give me the details." Doris turned on one side and faced Ruth.

"I am not thinking of anyone, Doris. It's been an eventful day, that's all. Now go to sleep." Ruth snapped her eyes shut, and hoped Doris would do the same.

"You are thinking about Cal Taylor aren't you? Isn't he the most handsome man? I wish he would ask me out, but he never does." Doris rattled on.

"No, I am not thinking about Cal Taylor." Ruth faced the wall and hoped Doris would get the hint.

"Then who, Ruth? I saw the look on your face. It's not *that* dark in here. We are going to be living together. I want to be your friend, so give. I want details."

Ruth sighed, turned back around, and sat up. "Okay, if you must know, his name is Peter…Peter Kirby. I was to marry to him, but another woman came in and swept him away."

The pig-tailed Doris popped up and stood in the middle of the room, her white flannel bed gown billowed in the draft from the window. "Married? Oh my gosh. You were to be married at seventeen? I am going to die. How romantic. Please, Ruth. Tell me all about it.

The two girls huddled cross-legged on one bed, and Ruth told the story of her arranged marriage, the rebellion, and eventual feelings of love for the man she did not want to marry. There were squeals of delight, moans of dismay, and they talked into the wee hours of the morning.

Dawn came too early, and they struggled to wake up and get ready for class.

"It was so worth it, though, Ruth. Nothing exciting happens to me. You've already had more excitement than most of the girls here. Don't worry, I will help you get through your first day." Doris promised.

Ruth went through the rest of the day in a sort of fog until she reached the home economics class. The thought of learning the secrets of the tastes and flavors of the culinary world awakened her senses. After class, Ruth headed for the dormitory room, but a voice from behind stopped her in the hall.

"Ruth, make I speak with you for a moment?" It was Cal.

"What are you doing here, Cal? Shouldn't you be working this time of day?" She glanced around the hall.

"Break. Can we step out in the courtyard? I would like to ask you something."
"Okay, but only a second. I didn't sleep very well last night, and I hoped for a small nap before dinner and homework." The courtyard was chilly, the wind had picked up a bit, and Ruth shivered.
Cal took his jacket off and placed it over her shoulders. "I'll make this quick. I don't want you to catch cold. There is an annual dance between the two schools Saturday night, and I wanted to ask you to be my date before any of the other boys got the chance. I have to help Mother act as chaperone, but there is no reason I can't enjoy it!"
"A dance?" She thought back to the fateful night she and Ginny sneaked out to meet the boys from the high school. In part, it was why she ended up at this boarding school. Did she really want to go to a dance? "I'm sorry Cal, but I don't want to go. I'm not interested at all. Thank you for the invitation, but you should ask one of the other girls. They all have a crush on you." She took off the heavy jacket and handed it back to Cal.
He reached out and retrieved the coat, but stopped Ruth as she turned toward the door. "Wait. I don't want all those other silly girls. I want to ask you. You're different. More grown up, mature." He reached out a hand.
Ruth laughed. "There must be other girls in the Senior Class you find interesting. You don't know anything about me. I'm new to this school."
"They push me, Ruth. Put themselves in front of me, preen and flirt. I am sick to death of it. You have not once flirted with me. You're more serious, more level

headed. Please? There is no pressure. It will not make you my girlfriend, but it *will* save me from all the others who throw themselves at me for the chance to go to the dance," he pleaded.

Ruth stopped and watched the anguish in his eyes. "Well, if you put it that way. I guess it wouldn't hurt. Okay, I'll go to the dance with you."

He smiled broadly. "Thank you so much, Ruth. I will be a perfect gentleman, I promise."

She laughed. "You better be, or I'll have to tell your mother."

Her first day at Barkley Women's School was over. She made it through, but as she lay on the bed, all she could think of was Peter. Was he married yet? Were they blissfully happy? She fell asleep with Peter's name on her lips.

Chapter Twenty-One

The day of the dance arrived, and Ruth sat at a small desk by the window while her roommate slept in the far bunk. The letter to Ginny was finished, and she licked the envelope, folded the sheet, and slipped it inside. She pulled out another piece of paper and started writing, "Dear Father and Mother." The pen hovered over the parchment. Unable to form a sentence that made any sense, she tapped the pen on the desk, repeatedly. A list, of sorts, sat in front of her of all the events that transpired since her arrival. It was hard to verbalize the emotions coursing through her body when it came to Mother and Father. Still angry with them for trying to arrange a marriage for her in the first place, it simmered underneath the surface. Happiness over their reconciliation, and the obvious shift in their relationship, entered into the mix. Of course, she wanted their happiness, but felt adrift on a lonely island.

The other emotion she tried to push out of her mind was of Peter. She had been shocked and betrayed when they met, but the attraction grew as time passed. His kiss and strong arms set her body a tingle. Nevertheless, he was to marry someone else. She must move on, begin to think of what she wanted to do with her life now.

The bunk behind her creaked as its occupant awoke. "What are you doing, Ruth?'

"Writing home, Doris."

"Who? Your parents, Peter?

"Certainly not Peter, silly. He is engaged to someone else, remember?"

"Oh pooh. Anyway, you have Cal now." Doris chortled.

"I most definitely do *not* have Cal. I am doing him a favor."

"If you say so, Ruth."

The girls passed the rest of the day catching up on laundry and working on their school projects due the next week. The hour approached when they needed to dress for the dance. There really was not much choice in what they would wear because it was required they wear school uniforms to any boy/girl event.

After brushing her bobbed hair into a sheen and applying a little rouge and lipstick, Ruth felt ready to go.

Doris, on the other hand, ran around like a silly goose, changing ribbons and applying make-up.

The housemother knocked on the door and informed them it was time to go.

They walked, as a group, the few blocks to the boys' campus chaperoned by their hall mothers. At the head of the line marched, Mrs. Taylor, Cal's mother.

The boys lucky enough to have dates lined one side of the walkway. The rest stood on the other side of the walk and followed tradition. The girls approached—if they liked anyone they would nod their head, and the boy would follow her into the hall. Those who didn't get a nod had to take their chances inside, along the stag line.

Ruth spotted Cal, and he rushed forward to greet her. He took an arm and led her into the gymnasium. The music was playing, and at the end of the gym, long tables loaded with food and beverages beckoned.

Cal asked her if she wanted a cold drink, and she said yes. While he was gone, Mrs. Taylor approached her. "Cal is a perfect gentleman, Ruth. Don't worry about him. It is good to see you are getting out and moving on with your life. The unpleasantness you left behind in Detroit will dim quickly as you focus on your future. Peter Kirby will become a thing of the past."

Shocked, Ruth responded, "How did you know about Peter? I didn't tell you about him."

"Oh my dear, you do not think we accept girls without knowing their background, do you? I knew about Mr. Kirby from the beginning."

Ruth continued to stare at the head mistress in disbelief.

Cal returned with a cold beverage. "What are you two talking about, Mother? Not me, I hope."

"No dear, not you," said Mrs. Taylor. "I must attend to my duties now. You two have fun."

"What were you talking about, Ruth?" He turned to hand her the glass.

She took the tumbler and stared into its depths. "Nothing, Cal. Really, nothing."

In the far corner of the room, a commotion broke out between a few of the girls. The scuffle continued to escalate, and Ruth wanted to move closer to check out the little skirmish.

Cal tried to discourage her.

"I want to see what the fight is about. It's the most excitement I've had since I arrived. Don't be such a killjoy, Cal." Ruth pulled him toward the pandemonium.

A nucleus of students surrounded two girls scratching and clawing each other, pulling hair, kicking, and screaming.

"You take that back," a red-faced blonde screamed, her yellow dress torn at the shoulder.

"I will not, you daughter of a scalawag and scoundrel. You don't belong here, and I want nothing to do with the likes of an offspring of Captain Adams," shouted a petite redhead, a tattered blue hair ribbon sat askance and dangled in front of her face.

Ruth stood rooted to the spot at the mention of the Captain. Adams? Could it be the same man?

Cal tried to tug her from the fray. "Let the chaperones deal with this, Ruth. This is none of our business."

She jerked away from him and moved nearer the scene. "I have to hear this. I have to know."

"Know what, Ruth?"

She didn't answer, only pushed closer to the crowd. When she turned around, he was gone. The two girls attended her home economics class, and she only knew their first names, Ella and Gretchen. She tried to figure out which one held the last name of Adams.

The chaperones finally broke up the fight, order returned, and the two offenders were whisked out of the dance. Ruth vowed to find out more about the mysterious girl with the last name of Adams. A quick glance around the room revealed Cal sulking against the far wall by the food table.

"What are you doing over here, Cal? You disappeared before I could ask you which one is an Adams, Gretchen or Ella."

"Why do you want to know those girls? They are both spoiled troublemakers. I'd hate to think you would associate yourself with shallow brats like those two." He grabbed a finger sandwich and stuffed it in his mouth, took a swig of punch, and turned a shoulder to her.

Ruth plucked at his sleeve. "I'm so sorry, Cal. I'm not interested in them as friends. It's a personal matter. One I am reluctant to talk about with anyone. It involves my parents and an incident twenty years ago. I really need to know which one is an Adams. Do you know? I promise I'll dance every dance with you."

Cal faced her and smiled. "Promise? Will you go to the Spring Cotillion with me, too? It's a much bigger deal than this little attempt at a dance. I don't want anyone to ask you before I get a chance."

She frowned, but thought over the prospects. Better to go with Cal, than some pimple-faced freshman. "Sure, it's a deal. Now which one is the Adams girl?"

"Ella, her name is Ella Adams. Don't get mixed up with her, she's rich, spoiled, and use to getting her way about everything. Not the kind of friend you need. Stick with Doris. She's real people." He took her arm and led her to the dance floor.

The music resumed and the previous clatter faded into a memory. "Who is her father, Cal? Is he a Captain? Captain Alexander Adams?" Ruth stopped moving to the music.

Cal wrinkled his brow and closed his eyes. "He's a Captain, all right, but I can't remember his first name. Just Captain Adams. Rich guy. Gives his daughter everything." He opened his eyes. "Not that she ever appreciates anything. From what Mother says, she just asks for more. Can we actually dance, now Ruth? I feel kind of silly just standing in the middle of the floor."

She smiled, although every fiber in her body wanted to leave the dance and track down this Ella Adams. They moved to the music, and Ruth realized Cal was an accomplished dancer. They fit rather well together, he was easy to follow, and she felt comfortable in his embrace. *Patience, Ruthie. He really doesn't know anything more, but I'm sure Doris does. I can ask her when I get back to the dorm.*

Ruth fulfilled her promise to Cal and danced the rest of the evening with him. She forced herself not to ask questions about the Adams girl and ended up having a very pleasant evening, Cal, ever the gentleman, escorted her safely to the door, brushed a kiss across her cheek, and said goodnight.

Back in the dorm, she rushed to find Doris—only the room was empty. *Doris must still be at the dance.* Restless, Ruth decided to walk through the hallways instead of wait in the room. Through the third upstairs hall, she passed room 302 and thought she heard someone crying. It took about fifteen minutes to make up her mind to knock on the door. The first knock was light, and there was no response. She gathered her courage and knocked louder. The door opened a crack, and Ruth found herself face to face with the feisty redhead from the dance. "Hi Gretchen, my name is Ruth, may I come in?"

Chapter Twenty-Two

Peter made good on his promise to make sure Hattie Morgenstern recovered completely from her twisted ankle. It hadn't swelled much, and once she knew it wasn't broken seemed to forget about it. He took her back to the boarding house and called on her the next day.

She assured him no doctor was required. "Would you like some refreshment, Peter? It's the least I can do."

"No thank you, Hattie. I must be on my way. I hope you won't hesitate to call if it takes a turn for the worst." He tipped his hat and started to back out of the doorway.

"Wait," she said. "What about our meeting, today? Did you get the appointment?"

He reached out and touched her hand. "Yes, yes, I most definitely did. I will come by for you at two pm. Right now, I need to go and talk to the Squires."

"You mean you haven't heard from them? They don't know?"

"No, nothing, nor have I caught them home. I can't imagine what is going on. The smart thing to do would be to camp out on their porch until I catch them, but I have a milk route to run." He started toward the front porch. "See you at two, Hattie."

A pang of sympathy stabbed his heart as he watched her wave from the porch. She was a nice girl, after all. Since her parents' deaths, she had to fend for herself. There were no suitable husband prospects in her hometown, and she did the only thing she knew to do.

He hoped the plan they hatched together in the garden last night worked for them both. *Nothing is going to work if I can't find Ruth. Where in the devil have they gone?*
The Squires' auto was parked at the front curb, and Peter's heart soared. *They are home, at last!* He bounded up the front steps and pounded the brass knocker. The sound reverberated up and down the street. He waited...no one came to the door. Again, he knocked. He checked the doorjamb and saw the paper he left the night before was gone. *They must have read the note. Why don't they answer?*
Not a sound came from the house. There was no movement at all. Finally, he could wait no longer. He climbed the perch on his milk wagon. The milk route could not be neglected. Duty called.

◆◆◆◆

Priscilla watched Peter through the parlor window. It broke her heart to watch the desperation on his face. Sarah found the note and waited for a private moment to give it to her. The note was sealed, and Priscilla felt confident Sarah hadn't read it.
The right thing to do was show her husband ... and Ruth, but she didn't. Jaw set, she lowered the curtain, and left the room. *This is the only way to make it right for my daughter. It was wrong to arrange a marriage of any kind for her. School is where she belongs. I will pay for this in the end, but I will have saved my daughter from a premature marriage. She will study and grow...meet new friends, and experience a completely new world.*
The house settled into its evening rhythm. The chime of the grandfather clock, the whispers of old boards settling, the wind kissing the curtains through the seams of the windows ... the life of a home.

Chapter Twenty-Three

Johnny the Nose thumbed through the money in the envelope Eric Horton handed him. The springs on his office chair chirped as he leaned back and stared at the ceiling.

"What a chump. Little does he know, I'm headed to Canada. He waltzes in here and hands me all this dough. Can anyone be more stupid? I ought to check out this Peter Kirby anyway, though. Hell, if I can't recruit the mug, I might put the squeeze on him. Might not hurt to check out the dame, too. Either way, I got that bag of shell's moola. Whatever way the situation turns out, I win."

He picked up the telephone and dialed. "Yeah, Moose…Johnny here. I gotta little job for ya."

◆◆◆◆

At precisely two o'clock in the afternoon, Peter arrived in front of the boarding house as promised. The front door opened, and Hattie stood dressed in her good, gray-blue dress, ready to go.

"Good morning, Ms. Morgenstern. You look very nice. Ready to go?" He offered an arm.

One gloved hand wound its way through his bent elbow, and side by side, they descended the steps. "I am very excited, Peter. I'm so glad you came up with this idea and relieved you know a banker who can draw up the agreement."

"Now, Hattie, I didn't say I know him well, and an unsettling change of events dictates I use another banker." He paused at her startled look. "Never fear, we will present our proposal and see what they say. If they refuse, we will seek another. I keep my promises."

"But, they *must* say yes. It's the perfect solution. Nothing has delighted me so much since I left the homeland." Hattie squeezed his arm. "To think I could have security, start a new life. It's rather breath-taking."

Peter smiled. "Let's not put the cart before the horse—one step at a time."

The bank was bustling...people coming and going, the lines at the tellers long. Peter maneuvered through the crowd toward the head teller.

"Hey, buddy, watch where you're going."

Peter's arm brushed across the shoulder of a man at the end of one line. "Excuse me, sir. I'm in a hurry. I didn't see you there."

"Yeah well, wait your turn." The man drew his jacket aside to reveal the butt of a gun, and closed it quickly.

Peter recognized the glint of steel and pulled Hattie in the opposite direction. "Today is not the day. We need to leave."

"But, why? We just got here. I'm counting on doing our business today." Hattie extracted her arm from Peter's grasp.

"Please, just follow my lead. Trust me, this *is not* a good day. We can go to another bank." Peter flinched as a hand clasped his shoulder.

"So, we meet again, Mr. Kirby. Who have we here? Is this your Ruth?" Eric Horton gave a sweeping bow. "I am at your service, no waiting."

"No, Mr. Horton, this is not Ruth, and we have come on other business. If you will excuse us..."

"Whatever business you have at this bank, I can help you with, Peter. Come to my office." Eric walked toward his office door.

"No, I think we need to see another loan officer." Peter steered Hattie away.

"Oh, no, I insist. I'd like to talk…"

"Hey Mac, this guy bothering you?" The gun-toting miscreant placed himself between Eric and Peter.

Horton's face drained of color.

"Not at all, sir. On second thought, maybe we should talk to you, after all, Mr. Horton." Peter backed away and gripped Hattie's arm.

Eric Horton, nonplussed, nodded, and scurried toward his office.

Hattie stomped a foot and wrenched her arm away. "What in blazes was that all about?"

"Please, the other man had a gun, Hattie."

"A gun?"

"Be quiet," Peter hissed. "The newspapers are full of sinister activities of various gangs in the city. Just be on your guard."

Hattie lowered her voice. "What gangs are you talking about?"

"I don't know. I believe they call themselves the Purple Gang. They run things around here. I've only read about them. The guy flashed the gun after I bumped into him. His clothes…well, he looks the part. Maybe we should leave."

A whiny voice hissed across the crowded foyer. "Kirby. Follow me, hurry…I don't have all day."

"Coming, Horton." Peter steered his charge toward the hall.

The officer of the bank led them down a window-lined hallway. Rows of typewriters behind the glass chattered away, women's fingers flying over the keys, bent to their work.

Peter squeezed Hattie's elbow. "Maybe you could get a job here."

"I can't type."

"Well, it was a thought."

The room on the other side of the hall contained rows of men in business suits talking into Dictaphones. Peter whispered in her ear. "I wonder if they do that all day. The confinement would not suit me, at all."

At the end of the hall, a door opened, and Eric ushered them into a very large, impressive office. Rich, wood wainscoting, large windows encased with heavy, moss green drapery, and leather chairs reflected the personality of the man Peter came to see.

"Horton, this isn't the office I was in last time. Did you get a promotion?"

"No, no, this is the Vice President's office. He is out of town. I didn't want everybody watching our business, if you know what I mean. This is more private."

"May I present Hattie Morgenstern." Peter gently pushed her forward.

"Exquisite to meet you, Miss Morgenstern." Eric bowed and kissed her hand. "Won't you have a seat?" Without another glance at Peter, he pulled a chair out. Once she was comfortable, he crossed the room to the large desk.

Hattie wrinkled her nose and whispered to Peter. "A bit arrogant isn't he?"

"Shh, we need to stay on his good side."

Hattie wasted no time in stating her purpose. "I'm here to procure a loan. I wish to buy a business."

"Yes, so Peter advised me when we spoke on the phone. My dear, I would truly like to accommodate you, but unfortunately, you are not a citizen of this country nor are you gainfully employed. The other matter concerns collateral."

Peter interrupted, "We've gone all over those points. I told you, I would be responsible for the loan if Ms. Morgenstern found herself unable to make payment."

"And a gallant offer, to be sure. One requirement, however, I cannot overlook. She has no income. Even though the boarding house offers revenue, the expenses will far out way any money brought in by boarders. A job is necessary."

"I've just come to this country, what should I do?" Hattie leaned forward and placed a hand on the top of the desk.

"What did you do in your country before you came here?" The banker sat back in his chair.

"I was a teacher."

"Ah, then, teach!"

"Where, sir?"

"I like you, Ms. Morgenstern. Let me make some inquiries. I have connections. Give me a few days, and I will phone you. Oh, by the way, Peter. Where *is* your Ruth? I haven't had the pleasure of meeting her. You never returned the papers I gave you. No trouble in paradise is there?" Eric held Peter's gaze, a sly smile twitched at the corner of his mouth.

Peter returned the stare. "Things have been postponed for a while. Unforeseen circumstances…you understand, I'm sure."

"Yes, I believe I do." Eric's smile widened. "I'm afraid I have another engagement. If you will excuse me?" He turned to Hattie. "I will call you in a few days Ms. Morgenstern."

"Fair enough. In the meantime, I will inquire at a few schools close by. Maybe they will transfer my certificate." Hattie rose.

Peter joined her and stopped at the door. "One more thing, the man in the lobby has a gun. I would be remiss if I didn't warn you."

"Yes well, I know the man. He actually guards the lobby most days to ward off any unsavory characters, if you know what I mean."

"Well, in that case, I have done my duty. Good day, sir."

The door closed behind them. Hattie frowned. "I'm not going to get the loan, am I?"

"I have no idea, but the atmosphere in the office turned cold after I mentioned the gun. Did you notice?" Peter hurried Hattie out the front door. "Maybe, we should go to another bank."

"Oh Peter, what am I to do? I'm afraid if I don't get the loan, I will have to hold you to the betrothal. I have no other recourse."

"Now Hattie, we will work it out. I promise. Let's not get ahead of ourselves. I say, there seems to be some commotion going on. Get in the automobile." Peter opened the passenger door.

A large, black vehicle had parked directly behind Peter's. He could hear an argument heating up between two very large men standing beside the shiny sedan

"But Johnny, I thought the Cap'n told us to off those two. No one told me about a change in orders. He's gonna take it out on me if I don't finish the job." The pug-faced goon, dressed in all black, flashed a revolver.

A tall, large-nosed fellow flicked lint from his pinstriped suit and stepped from behind the gunman. "You heard me, Moose. I get my orders directly from the Captain. That's a fact, and you know it." The man wrenched the pistol from the thug. "Case of mistaken identity, see. We get paid to protect the bank, that's all." He stuffed the weapon in a suit pocket, flashed a look at Peter, and tipped his hat.

Peter dodged the eye contact and scrambled into the automobile. "Let's get out of here."

"I heard what those men said. The city is so dangerous. Is it always like this in the States? Who is to protect me when you marry Ruth?" She dabbed her eyes with a rumpled handkerchief.

He steered the auto toward the boarding house, but remained silent. A block from the bank he finally took a breath. "Don't cry, Hattie. I will make sure you get the loan. No need to enter into a marriage neither of us wants."

Hattie looked at Peter. "I don't want to make you unhappy, but I have few choices left. I want that boarding house, Peter."

◆◆◆◆

Hattie waved at him from the front door, and he rounded the corner for home. The Squires had not returned his messages or phone calls. Desperate at the possibility of losing Ruth, he made a quick decision to try their home once more, reversed his direction, and headed for town. The house had a look of abandonment. The drapes were drawn; no light twinkled through the shrouded windows. It was as if all life disappeared from the once vibrant home. His heart sank. *Where could they have gone?*

Despite the obvious, Peter ran up the steps and rapped the doorknocker against the thick door, and the hollow sound echoed, forlorn, and hopeless. *How can I find her? She cannot have just disappeared into thin air. If I could only talk to Sarah, I know she would tell me.* He stood, helpless, until finally, he backed away from the door, and returned to his auto.

◆◆◆◆

The horses whinnied from the barn, but Peter ignored their pleas. *Maybe Mother has heard from them. If only…*

"Peter!" Elizabeth called from behind the house. "Are you back already?" She hurried toward him, wiping her hands on a dishtowel. "Did she get the loan?"

He shook his head. "Not yet, Horton is making inquiries. We'll know in a few days."

"Horton? Eric Horton? Isn't he the banker that wants to marry Ruth? Why would you deal with him? Surely, there are other loan officers."

"Believe me, I didn't want to deal with him, but a strange occurrence at the bank forced me to make a snap decision. A man flashed a gun in the lobby, a type of gangster, I think. Eric Horton was visibly upset, he practically begged me to follow him. Since I was responsible for Hattie's safety, I decided to take him up on the offer."

Elizabeth's hand flew to cover her mouth. "Peter, a gangster? What is this city coming to? A respectable citizen is not safe anymore. Poor Hattie. Was she terrified?"

"She didn't see the gun, but I told her about it. I thought she handled it well. Horton assured her he would make inquiries into employment for her since that is a requirement. I can only hope he's a man of his word." He removed his coat and hat and hung them in the entrance of the house. "There were more men outside talking about taking out two people, but one of them convinced the other it was a mistake. I hustled Hattie into the auto and hurried away."

"Oh my goodness…"

"Mother, have you heard from the Squires or Ruth? I am beside myself with worry. Where can she be?" Peter sank down on a chair in the kitchen.

"No, not a word."

"Hattie threatened to hold me to the betrothal if she doesn't get the loan. I have to find Ruth."

"We'll find her, dear. Don't give up. They cannot have just vanished from the earth. Let me finish your supper. The boys will return from the neighbors, soon, hungry and rambunctious." She laid a hand on his back. "Why don't you go out and bed the horses for the evening. It will be dark soon, and it's going to be a cold night."

He patted her hand and heaved himself from the chair. "You're right. I should have done it before I came in. I am so tired and empty inside, but no reason to neglect the horses. I'll be right back."

Under the dusky sky, Peter raised his face in supplication. "Please Lord, help me find her. I need her in my life."

The brush made a raspy sound as he curried the old friends…long, slow strokes. He wasn't sure how long he stayed in the barn, but when his mother found him, he sat on a hay bale, the brush in one hand, staring into space. Night had fallen.

Chapter Twenty-Four

Gretchen McGrath dabbed her eyes and peered at Ruth. "I know you. Home economics, you are the new girl. What do you want?"

"I will be honest; you made quite a spectacle at the dance. Ella Adams…I want to talk about her." Ruth placed a foot over the threshold.

"What's it to you? Leave me alone." The girl tried to shut the door.

"Look, give me a minute. Ella is no friend of mine. It's her father I want to ask about—a personal matter." The door stopped at Ruth's shoe.

"Well …"

Ruth eased into the room and glanced around. "I don't want to bother you, really. It looked like a nasty fight. Are you hurt?"

"No, only my pride. Ella makes me crazy. I know I shouldn't let her get to me, but this time …" Gretchen flopped down on the bed.

"So, Captain Adams is her father?"

"I wouldn't admit to it if I was her, but yes, she's the offspring of the scalawag. Why do you want to know?"

Ruth continued to stand in the middle of the room. "My mother…had dealings with him before I was born. I'm trying to find out if this Captain Adams is the same one. Would his first name be Alexander?"

Gretchen jumped up, grabbed a tissue, and blew her nose. "Yep, that's him. Maybe you should leave. I'm not sure I want to associate with someone who rubs elbows with the likes of him."

"No, you don't understand. He hurt my mother. I want revenge."

Gretchen's green eyes assumed the gleam of a lioness on the hunt. "In that case, you can stay. I would like nothing better than to destroy that little tramp, and if her father goes down too, so much the better. Here, sit down." She cleared a spot on the rumpled bed. "Where do you want me to start?"

◆◆◆◆

The night air coaxed Cal Taylor to walk slowly and savor the crispness of the late, winter evening. At first, he was frustrated about his inability to sway Ruth to take an interest in him, but he was no fool. Clearly, her heart pined for a lost love.

Even his mother foretold the drama in Ruth's past. "Cal, hers is the face of a woman betrayed, yet love remains. Watch yourself, you might get hurt. Take someone else to the dance, dear. Save yourself the trouble."

Naturally, he didn't listen, but smiled broadly remembering Ruth's acceptance of the little peck on the cheek at the door. "Oh well, she will make a great friend, someone I can talk to on my level, not like the other giggling girls."

The long, winding, shrub-lined walkway from the administration building served as a favorite hangout for the girls. Most of the time you could see clusters of two or three reclined on blankets or the concrete benches. Unfortunately, the January weather discouraged this activity, especially late in the evening. Cal enjoyed the leisurely stroll, but slowed at an unexpected sight near the entrance gate. A man, both hands stuffed in the pockets of a heavy tweed jacket paced back and forth outside the fenced area. The wool, flat cap and the shadow of a beard gave him a rough look. Cal hung back, slowed his gait … waiting.

In an abrupt movement, the enigmatic fellow spun on his heel, leered at him, and walked briskly to the corner. The stranger hesitated only moment, touched a finger to his cap, and disappeared.

Uneasy, Cal changed his destination and returned to his mother's office.

"It is unusual, to say the least, Cal, but we are well guarded. Would you feel better if you stayed on campus tonight—maybe in the gardener's shack? He's gone home for the winter." Mrs. Taylor rummaged in the old desk drawer and withdrew a brass ring crowded with an agglomeration of keys. She thumbed through several until nimble fingers singled out the one of choice.

"Good idea, Mother. I am a bit jumpy, I guess, but something about his look gave me a bad feeling. I have never seen a mobster, but if I had to imagine one, he is what I would envision. Why would someone like him be in this neighborhood? We're not in the city." Cal took the key from her hand.

"This wouldn't have anything to do with Ruth would it?" The bright smile lit the twinkle in her eyes.

"No, tonight I realized Ruth is in love with another. I consider her a friend. She doesn't giggle, if you know what I mean."

"I imagine she was a typical, giggly teenage girl not too very long ago, Cal. Her heart is broken. Watch yours, young man." Mrs. Taylor closed the drawer and turned off the office light. "I'm going home, the dance wore me out. Not sure how many more years I can do this. I'm not young anymore."

"I'll walk you to the car, Mother. Remember to wake me up in the morning…and bring me some biscuits and gravy." He hugged her and watched the automobile disappear into the night.

The old shack offered few comforts. A rickety wooden bed stood in the corner and a washbasin beside it.

"All the comforts of home." Cal sighed deeply and settled in for the night under the homemade quilt. He wondered if the gardener's wife had stitched the beautiful bedcover. "Will I ever find a wife who thinks as much of me?"

◆◆◆◆

The little gardener's shack on the far side of the campus became the agreed location for the rendezvous with Ella Adams. Ruth convinced Gretchen to slip quietly out of the dormitory, push a note under Ella's door, and run. Ruth was to lay in wait at the little shanty for her victim to arrive. Once inside, Gretchen would bolt the door from the outside, and listen for Ruth's signal to let them out.

In her haste, Ruth never gave the need for a key a second thought. The run-down shack always looked abandoned and more like a storage building than someone's abode. Panic gripped her when she turned the knob. It wouldn't move. "Oh no, I don't have a key. Ella will be here any minute. Maybe there's a window open."

The grime-smeared windows offered no help. It looked like they were painted shut. Every window the same, Ruth went back to the door and rattled the knob again.

"Who's there?" The door opened with an ominous creak.

The door swung wide, and Ruth barely suppressed a scream. "Cal Taylor, what are you doing in this old shack?"

"I think the more intriguing question is…what are *you* doing here, Ruth? Come in here, you will catch your death of cold." He pulled her inside.

"I…I was going to meet a friend, but she's not coming so I'll just go…"

Cal held her firm. "Hold on, not so fast. What friend? Her name, please."

"Are you the campus police? I don't have to tell you anything. Let me go."

Through the door, Ruth heard a scream and muffled voices. "What is going on out there?"

Cal and Ruth bolted through the door together in time to see a shadow drag a struggling girl into the woods.

"Oh my God, someone has Ella. Who is that man?"

"Hey you," Cal shouted.

Ruth watched him run down the path. "What have I done?"

Cal stumbled back through the door, panting. "He's gone…with Ella. They sped off in an automobile. Need to find police."

"Who would take Ella, Cal? I never wanted this to happen. I wanted information, that's all. What have I done?"

Cal's breathing slowed. "This is your doing? You were meeting Ella? I told you to stay away from her. She is bad news."

"I'm sorry. I only wanted to talk to her. Gretchen helped me trick her to come to the shack." Ruth wrung her hands and paced the room, real fear pounding its cadence in her head.

"Never mind that now. We have to call the police and get in touch with her father. And how am I going to break the news to Mother?" Cal took Ruth by the hand and sprinted toward the administration building.

Within thirty minutes, the campus lit up like a Christmas tree with police scouring the grounds for clues. Ruth sat in the office, shaking, while detectives grilled her about the incident. Mrs. Taylor tried to shield her from the interrogation, but they were relentless.

Gretchen entered the scene with two police behind her. "I knew you were bad news, Ruth. I should have slammed the door in your face. Now look what you've gotten me into."

"Knock it off, Gretchen. You were more than willing to get in on the little scheme. I never meant for *this* to happen. How was I to know someone was after her?" Ruth turned away.

One of the police officers angled two chairs on either side of Mrs. Taylor's desk and insisted the girls sit. They fired questions at them, over and over, and spent almost an hour corroborating their stories.

Ruth fought back tears and exhaustion. Gretchen repeatedly blamed Ruth. Mrs. Taylor tried to calm both girls with little success. The phone rang in the middle of the fray. Mrs. Taylor answered.

"Mrs. Squire? Why, Ruth is here—what do you mean you got a ransom note? It wasn't your daughter, they got Ella. Please calm down, I can't understand..."

A rotund detective in a wrinkled trench coat grabbed the receiver from the school matron. "When did you receive this note? How did it arrive?" He scribbled furiously on a notepad.

Ruth jumped up and grabbed Mrs. Taylor's hand. "It's Mother? Why is she calling here? Have they heard the news of the kidnapping already?"

"My dear, they think it was you who was taken. A note arrived on their doorstep. It said they had you and wanted $10,000 for your return." Mrs. Taylor squeezed Ruth's hand. "I'm as confused as you."

Ruth took a step back, shaken. "Me? Why would anyone want me?"

The detective held the phone away from his ear and faced her. "Sounds like a case of mistaken identity. I'm sending a dispatch of men to your home to question your parents. You're in a lot of trouble, miss. Take the phone and calm down your mother." He shoved the phone at Ruth.

Her hand trembled as she took the receiver. "Mother? Yes, it's me. I am okay. Please, don't shout…I don't know why someone would want to kidnap me. Is Father there? May I talk to him?" After a short pause, Ruth smiled into the phone. "Father? Come take me home, I'm frightened." She shook her head. "No, I don't want to stay here. What if they come back when they find out Ella isn't me? Please, Father."

Mrs. Taylor encircled Ruth's shoulders. "Maybe it is best you stay here until we get to the bottom of all this nonsense."

"She must stay here," the rumpled detective interrupted. "She needs to be under our protection. We've witnessed other abductions in recent months. Seems to be a rash of them. Gang related, mostly. Extortion. It would be easier to keep an eye on her here. I can put a detail on Miss Squire's room, post a guard at her door."

"Father, they want to keep me prisoner. Please come and get me." Ruth pleaded.

The investigator folded his notepad and motioned for Ruth to hand him the phone. "Mr. Squire, we will take good care of your daughter, but if you would like to come here, that would be fine, too. Yes, I will await your decision. You can call Mrs. Taylor when your mind is made up. Don't worry, we will take good care of her."

Mrs. Taylor nodded. "Certainly, it makes perfect sense. I'm sure it will calm the other parents to know we have detectives on campus. Let me get Cal to walk you to your room." She paused and looked around the room. "Cal? Now, where has he gone? This is no time to disappear. I need him."

"Said he had some business to take care of, Mrs. Taylor. He left a few minutes ago. Don't worry about Miss Squire, my men will see her to the dorm."

"What about Ella, detective? How will you find her?"

"There is a massive search going on already. Please don't worry."

The room cleared of officers, and Ruth paused in front of the school matron. "I am so sorry, Mrs. Taylor. No harm was intended for anyone. I only wanted to speak to Ella about her father. Once again, I have made a mess of things."

"Sometimes, my dear, the most innocent of ideas can turn a world upside down. Don't worry about it. We will find Ella."

"What about me?" Gretchen whined from the chair by the desk. "What if they come back for me?"

"Oh my, I almost forgot about you, Miss McGrath. What shall we do with you? You were confined to your room, if you remember, for the little commotion at the dance. I believe we will extend your punishment. Return to your room and stay there until further notice. No one is after you. It's safe there."

"Before I leave, Gretchen, I want to apologize for my part in this. I was so hell-bent on revenge; I dragged you into this mess. Mrs. Taylor, I am the instigator. Gretchen shouldn't be punished for something I started." Ruth saw the surprise in the girl's face at her announcement.

"Nevertheless, Gretchen's infraction started at the dance, and she alone decided to continue. Your attempt to get her off the hook is noted: the rest is in the hands of the school board. Good night, Ruth."

Chapter Twenty-Five

The city skyline twinkled on the horizon, and Cal began to doubt his decision to find Peter Kirby. "I should have told Mother my plan…or more accurately, the skeleton of a plan. Maybe I didn't think this through. Although, if Ruth is the intended target of the kidnapper, it means she is still in danger. The man she loves needs to know. I imagine her parents won't tell him, after all, they whisked her away to school."

The streetlights offered a welcoming glow, but did little to assure the growing apprehension. A quick scan of the area discouraged him even more. Businesses stood shuttered at this time of night. "How do I find Peter Kirby?"

He drove another mile and saw a quaint shingle swinging in the evening breeze. The post stood by the roadway in invitation. "Ah, maybe Mrs. Whitewood's Boarding House could offer assistance." Cal pulled the motorcar into the narrow driveway.

A soft glow illuminated the front window, even though the hour was late. Cal picked his way carefully along the sidewalk, careful not to disturb the pink blooms on the creeping roses lining the walk. "The hour *is* very late—but, there is a light, so someone must be awake." He lifted the small doorknocker and gave it a quick rap. Almost at once, the porch light beamed overhead. Cal jumped.

The frosted-glass door opened slowly. "Yes? I only have one room left, young man. Do you want it or not?" A stooped, white-haired woman, leaning on a cane, peered up at Cal's face.

He snatched the cap from his head. "Uh…well, I don't know…I mean, I'm looking for someone, but I might need a room. It's too late to find him tonight, I suspect."

"Yes, or no, mister, I'm an old woman. I don't have time to stand here blabbering. Hattie, you can check in the bloke. It is going be your business soon anyway. I'm going to bed." The old lady spun around and thumped down the hallway.

"I apologize, sir. She is a cranky thing, at times. I have only been here a few days, myself. I believe she is more than ready to retire." Hattie opened the door wider and stepped to the side.

Cal hesitated, but weary to the bone, decided the boarding house was the answer for the night. "Thank you, I don't mean to disturb so late, but I just realized how tired I am. If there is a room, I would like to have it. Let me introduce myself. My name is Cal Taylor."

"Certainly, come in, Mr. Taylor. I am Hattie Morgenstern. Let's get you settled." She pointed to a small desk by the window. "Please sit over there. A bit of refreshment will soothe the weariness. The sideboard is in the corner."

"You are very kind." He watched the slender woman arrange the tea service on a silver tray, and admired her carriage and polished appearance.

"I heard you tell Mrs. Whitewood you were looking for someone." She handed him a cup of steaming tea.

Careful not to spill the hot liquid, Cal set the cup on the side table. "Yes, maybe you could help me."

Hattie shook her head, settled in the chair opposite him, and took tiny sips from the delicate cup. "I'm afraid not, Mr. Taylor. I have only been here a few days. I don't know anyone in the city."

"You came to a strange city alone?" Cal was tired, but something about the young woman intrigued him.

"Unfortunately, there is nothing left for me in my homeland. It's a matter of survival now." Her gaze fixed on something in the distance.

Cal hesitated. "I'm sorry. I don't mean to pry, but why did you pick this place?"

"My betrothed is here."

A surprise pang of disappointment shot through him. "You are going to be married?"

"I was…it's been called off for now. It's really rather complicated. What about you? Where do you live?" Her eyes refocused, and she smiled.

"Not much to tell. I work for a women's boarding school. My mother is the headmistress there. I received my degree two years ago, but I haven't found any other work. I want to open a store of some kind. Money is the issue, I'm afraid." The warm tea made him sleepy after all the excitement at the school. *If I don't lay down pretty soon, I might pass out.*

"Cal, you look like you could go to sleep on the spot. How very rude of me. I'll show you to your room, and you can get a fresh start in the morning." She took the cup from his shaking hand and retreated to the stairs. "Come this way. You need sleep."

He followed like a young pup, unable to argue. *In the morning…I'll find him in the morning.*

◆◆◆◆

The hour was late when Ruth and the officer arrived at the door of her room. *It didn't take me long to mess up everything at the school. Mother is right; I am headed down a dangerous path.* She expected to see Doris already in bed, but the bunk was neat as a pin and her roommate was nowhere in sight.

Ruth spun around. "What happened to Doris, officer? Why isn't she here?"

"Ms. Taylor thought it best to relocate her to a different room for now. Wouldn't do to get her mixed up in this. It's safer for all concerned. Don't fret, I'll be right outside the door." He stepped into the hall and closed the door.

"Why is it I always find myself locked in a room alone? Now they have taken Doris away from me. How do I get into these messes?" The rickety bunk squeaked at her weight. "One little infraction, climbing out my bedroom window cost me everything. Well, they aren't gonna keep me locked up this time."

Chapter Twenty-Six

Ella Adams struggled against the restraints, which bound both hands behind her back. The kidnapper blindfolded her, stuffed a handkerchief in her mouth, and tossed her onto the floorboards of the motorcar's back seat. She tried to make out what the driver was muttering about, but couldn't understand a word. *This has to be Ruth's doing. She lures me out to that shack and knew I would be assaulted. But why? I haven't done anything to her.*

The driver turned around. "Shut up, back there. It ain't gonna do you no good to feud and scream. No one can hear ya. Might as well enjoy the ride, Ruth. Time to worry when you see the boss."

Ruth? He thinks I'm Ruth? My God, he took the wrong girl. How am I going to convince him I'm not her? Ella stopped tussling and tried to formulate a plan. *Okay, Ella, don't panic. You look nothing like Ruth. I'm blonde, she has black hair. Once he realizes the mistake, he will let me go. I have no way to prove I'm not Ruth, but surely by the description he'll figure it out. It's my only chance.*

The automobile continued to speed down the long highway, and Ella lost track of time. Her shoulders burned from the unfamiliar position, and both wrists were raw from the rope binding. Unable to comprehend how long she lay bound and gagged, sleep rescued her from constant panic.

◆◆◆◆

The wharf was dark and empty. Johnny the Nose waited inside a shadowy passageway for the motorcar to flash its lights—a signal the job was successful. They had her. The boss would be pleased.

The girl looked unconscious as the two men pulled her out of the auto. "She better still be alive, you lunkheads. I wouldn't want to be you if she's not." He held the door open.

"Aw, she's passed out, Johnny. I don't kill 'em 'til the boss tells me. Where is he?" The hired men held the limp girl between them.

"Up those stairs, he'll be here in about an hour. In the meantime, you better get her cleaned up and presentable. You know how he likes 'em to look proper before he offs 'em."

"Why's he want to waste a pretty number like her? She don't look like no threat to me." The kidnapper lifted her chin and ran a hand over her cheek.

"How do I know? I don't question the jobs; I like the payola too much. Don't touch the merchandise, you fool. He might just want her for his own pleasure." Johnny watched them haul the girl up the stairs. *Guess I should wait down here 'til the boss gets here. Gotta take credit for the job getting done.*

Johnny pulled an old wooden chair against the open door, leaned it back on two legs, and kept vigil. He filed his nails, flicked lint from the pinstriped suit, combed his hair, and counted the money he received from this job. Not only did he clean up from Eric Horton, but the boss actually paid him double to kidnap her. Of course, he hadn't mentioned the money Horton gave him to the boss. He wasn't that stupid.

At the end of the alleyway, Johnny saw headlights turn in—the boss had arrived. The auto moved slowly, and he knew the driver took great care, making sure rival gangs didn't ambush them. Finally, the motorcar stopped right in front the doorway.

Johnny stood and kicked the chair behind him. "Evenin' boss, been expectin' ya."

A tall, well-dressed gentleman emerged.

"Whoa, boss. You been to some fancy affair? Never seen you in black tie before. Looks good on ya, though." Johnny scanned his boss from the shiny, black shoes to his slicked down hair

"Never mind that. Did you accomplish the job I gave you to do?" The man drew a white handkerchief from his breast pocket and wiped it across one brow.

"Sure did, boss, got her right up stairs. Wasn't no trouble at all."

"Good. I already paid you, so take her to the wharf, and tie a concrete block to her feet. I don't want to be seen down here. I can't be connected to this operation at all." He retreated to the auto.

"Wait, boss. You ain't even gonna look at her? She's a right pretty thing, blond ringlets, big blue eyes. Talk to her sweet and you might have a new little conquest. Bet she'd really go for a man of your stature. You can hide her in Canada, no one would look there." Johnny tossed coins in the air as he spoke.

The fancy man jerked around and grabbed Johnny by the lapel. "Blond hair? Blue eyes? The girl I wanted you to kidnap has black hair and brown eyes! Good God, what have you done?" He took the stairs two at a time, Johnny on his heels.

◆◆◆◆

Ella regained consciousness as the men tied her to a chair. One of them tried to brush the scattered curls into place with his fingers, while the other wiped her face with a wet cloth. She struggled to elude them both.

"Hey missy, you wanna look good for the boss, don't ya? He might even take a fancy to ya. You could do a lot worse. Hold still."

"Look you dolts. I heard you call me Ruth in the car. You have the wrong girl. My name is Ella. I know the girl you are looking for, and I can take you to her. I am *not* Ruth." She struggled against the bindings and tried to wrench away from their clammy hands.

"Nice try, Ruthie. We don't make mistakes like that." The taller thug tweaked her nose, while the other made sure the rope stayed tight.

She jerked her head away from the greasy fingers. "You idiots! My father is a very important man. Mess with me and you will have to tangle with him, and believe me, it won't be pleasant. Now let me go."

Footsteps clattered up the stairs, and all three swiveled around.

"Must be the boss. Sounds like he's in a big hurry."

Ella heard cursing, shouts of anger, and the thunder of heavy shoes ascending the wooden stairs like a herd of elephants, and anger melted into fear. She looked at her captors. Their eyes were wide, faces white. *They are afraid, too.* An uncontrollable shaking took over her body.

The door burst open and three men scrambled into the room.

Ella screamed.

Chapter Twenty-Seven

A spark of the old rebellious Ruth rose out of desperation, and the taste of escape washed over her at the dorm window. *I won't be locked in this room while someone else decides my fate. I have to save Ella.*

A delivery truck pulled down the long driveway in front of the school and disappeared around the back. *The night delivery! My one and only chance. Let's see if they lock the windows at this school.* The wood framed pane lifted easily and slid all the way to the top. The only problem—she was two stories high. A quick glance at the grounds and a plan formed. She swung a leg out the window, grabbed the largest branch of the sycamore tree next to the building, and eased out. Once settled in the tree, she carefully shimmied to the ground. The shadows obscured her presence while she tiptoed around the corner.

Detroit Laundry was printed on the side panel of the truck. *I'm in luck! They are delivering the weekly linen supply, and I know they will return to the city tonight. It's my fault Ella was taken. Eric Horton did this. I just know it.*

Ruth peeked around the corner of the administration building and waited for a chance to climb into the back of the laundry truck. *It's the only way to get back to the city. I have to find Eric Horton. He hired someone to kidnap me. Poor Ella, I never meant for this to happen. Only I can make it right.*

The deliverymen carried the fresh linens into the back door, and Ruth saw her opportunity. Just as she stepped onto the graveled drive, a hand clamped her forearm.

"What are you doing, Ruthie, trying to run away again?"

Ruth jumped, ready to strike the assailant. "Father! You scared me to death. I thought it was the kidnapper. What are you doing here?" She pulled him back into the shadows.

Robert Squire wrapped both arms around her. "I came to see about you. This is a dangerous situation, and you shouldn't have to deal with it alone."

"They locked me in my room. I can't go through that again. Ella is in danger, and it is my fault. I am trying to find a way back to the city to help her." She glanced back at the truck and saw the one opening slip away. The drivers were back and closing the bay door.

"Well, I agree, you shouldn't be locked up. Tell you what. I will drive you back, but you must promise me to break this habit of running away. Your mother and I can't take it anymore." He smiled and chucked her under the chin.

"Oh Father, would you? I promise it's the very last time."

"Let's go, the motorcar is over there." He pointed toward the tree-lined drive. "Don't you think you should tell someone you are leaving?"

Ruth grabbed his hand and raced toward the auto. "No one will miss me. I am going to find Ella. They will only try to stop me."

After a mad scramble across the lawn, they piled into the vehicle.

"I feel like a school boy again, skipping class. What would Mother say?" He laughed and steered away from the campus. "Now why don't you tell me how you got in this mess and why poor Ella figures into the picture?"

The hour and a half ride back home passed quickly. Ruth related the entire story as the trees and houses passed by the windows like a silent movie. Robert nodded and commented on each point, but fell quiet when the story turned to Ella.

"I know it was wrong to lure her to the gardener's shack, Father. Honestly, I only wanted to talk to her. The fact is you don't realize how she ties to our family." Ruth faced forward, unwillingly to witness the shock that would register on his face. "Her father is Captain Alexander Adams."

The steering wheel jerked to the left, and the auto lurched.

Ruth braved a glance at her father. "So you do know him."

Mr. Squire's mouth opened and closed, but no sound came out.

She reached over and touched his arm. "It's all right, Father. You see, I have known about him for quite a while. I just couldn't find time to talk to you about it. Mother doesn't know I'm aware of her past, either."

"How … who told …?"

"The letters, I found the letters and read them all." The pain on his face cut like a knife, but he had to know. Maybe together they could figure out how to save Ella.

"It's a shame you had to find out that way, Ruthie. I suppose we should have told you ourselves, but your mother and I actually did fall in love. We put the unpleasant memory behind us. So, that is why you wanted to talk to Ella—because of Mother?"

All she could do was nod.

"Mother had those letters burned, child. I saw her give them to Sarah ..." Color drained from his face.
"Father, please don't blame Sarah. She only hid them for Mother's protection from that horrible man. The torn ball gown is hidden away, as well."
Shadows zipped by under the starlit night, and the motor chugged along, the only sound, except for the labored breathing of the man beside her. It upset her to hurt him, but things had gone too far. If they were to save Ella, he must know the whole story. "I'm sorry, Father."
"It's not your fault. Ella is the one paying for her father's roguish behavior, poor child. What can we do, Ruthie? We cannot run in and tear her away from the captors. Do you know who is responsible or where they took her?"
Lights from the city dotted the horizon, she didn't have much time. "I think I do, Father. Eric Horton. He must be the one. Oh, he hired someone to do his dirty work, but he is behind it. Denied the prize, he will stop at nothing to get what he wants. We'll go to his house and confront him. I wouldn't be surprised if Ella was tied up in his basement."
The auto slowed. "I think we should go to the police first. We're not equipped to handle this alone."
"No, Father. He might become desperate and shoot his way out. I'll be able to tell by his face if he's hiding her. Please?"
"All I can promise is, we knock on his door—see what he does. Anything else, we get the police."
I'm lucky to get that much from Father. Can't rock the boat now. "That is all I ask. Thank you, Father. Do you know where Horton lives?"

He gave a curt nod. The rest of the trip passed in silence until they rolled into the banker's street.

"Are you sure about this, Ruthie?"

The deepening wrinkles in his face, and the sadness of his eyes didn't escape Ruth's notice, but she must find out. "It will be all right, Father. Wait in the motorcar for me. I will find out if he is here."

The walkway to Eric Horton's front door stretched ahead endlessly.

◆◆◆◆

"Good morning, Mr. Taylor. I trust you slept well. Breakfast is ready, come right on into the kitchen." Hattie pointed to the doorway.

Cal felt drugged by the fitful sleep of the previous night, but the smell of bacon and hotcakes revived his spirit. "Oh my, it smells so good. I hope there is some strong coffee made."

"It's a chicory blend, Cal. Glad to know you enjoy a morning cup. I don't think I could start my day without it." Hattie poured the black liquid into a large mug.

"Come on, come on, young man. I'm about to starve. Don't keep an old woman waiting for breakfast. I have to get into town today to buy supplies." Mrs. Whitewood sat at the table tapping her fork on the china plate.

"I'm so sorry, Mrs. Whitewood." He sat down and reached for the hot brew.

"Never mind, now tell us about yourself and who you are looking for."

His mouth watered at the sight of the fluffy flapjacks in front of him, but swallowed hard, and smiled at the owner of the boarding house. "I made the trip from

Barkley's School for Women to find a gentleman who is involved with a student of ours. It's a long story, but I fear she is in danger, and I thought he could help."

"Barkley's School for Women? Is it far from here? I'm looking for a position as a teacher. Maybe they have an opening." Hattie held her fork in midair. "I plan to buy the boarding house, but they won't give me a loan unless I am gainfully employed. You say the young woman is in danger?"

"Yes, there was a kidnapping at the school last night. It's most bizarre because they took Ella instead. A case of mistaken identity I'm afraid." Cal wolfed down a couple of bites.

"Kidnapping? At the school? Who would do such a thing?" Hattie stopped eating and lay down her utensil.

"The detectives think it is gang related, probably wanted to get the daughter of a prominent citizen in exchange for money. Extortion, you know. I've never known the mob to come out that far though."

Hattie gasped. "Gangs...why we encountered such a thing in town yesterday—right by our automobile. They had guns and everything. The poor girl. Do you think they will kill her?"

"I am not familiar with the way they operate. The girl is in danger, I know that much." He took the last bite, swallowed the last of the coffee, wiped his mouth, and stood. "Now ladies, if you will excuse me, I must be going."

"I know you are in a hurry, Cal. It's really been a pleasure talking with you. I hope we see each other again." Hattie stood and followed him into the foyer.

"You've been most kind, Ms. Morgenstern." He bowed toward the old woman. "And you as well, Mrs. Whitewood." A wrinkled piece of paper fell out his coat pocket. "Oh, I almost forgot, can either of you tell me where to find this address? I need to talk with the girls' parents."

Hattie shook her head. "I'm not familiar with the town. Mrs. Whitewood?"

Cal motioned for the woman to stay seated and hurried to her side. "If you could point me in the right direction, maybe I could find the young man."

"Oh yes, I know exactly. My nephew lives on the same street. If you will take me to town, young man, I'll show you." The grandfather clock in the hall sounded eight o'clock. "We must hurry, though. The day is getting away from us."

"Wonderful, but how will you get home? I might not be coming back this way." Cal worried.

"Ms. Whitewood has an auto. My plan was to look for work in the city today, but I'm not ready. Why don't you go on with her, and I'll meet you later at the bank. I can pick her up there." Hattie looked at both of them.

"Great idea. Ready to go, Ms. Whitewood?" Cal asked.

"I was born ready, sonny. What are you waitin' on?"

◆◆◆◆

Cal Taylor followed Mrs. Whitewood's directions and parked in front of Robert and Priscilla Squire's brownstone. His passenger requested to visit her nephew in the next block, so he delivered her safely to the door and continued his mission—find Peter Kirby. A quick knock and the door swung open immediately.

"Yes, do ya have news? Are ya from the bureau?" A small woman in maid's attire addressed him. An Irish brogue rolled off her tongue.

Cal snatched the cap from his head. "Pardon me, no, I'm not from any bureau. I am from Barkley's Women's School. Could you tell me where to find Peter Kirby?"

The maid stood with mouth open for a moment. "The school? Where Miss Ruthie goes?"

"Yes, Ruth Squire. She is in danger, and I'm looking for Peter. Can you help me?"

She shook her head. "I cannot, but if you will wait a moment, I'll fetch Mrs. Squire."

The door closed in his face. He waited and tried to peer through the glass to see if anyone would return.

Two minutes went by, and the door opened again…slowly. "Who did you say you are, sir? From the school?"

Cal gazed at the stout woman holding on to the door handle. "My name is Cal Taylor. Are you Ruth's mother? Ma'am, she is in danger. I would like to talk to you about Peter Kirby. She talks about him all the time. I know she is in love with him, and maybe he could help protect her. I was in the office when you called. You *know* they kidnapped the wrong girl. They wanted Ruth. Peter needs to know."

"Come in, young man. The detectives are here. You should talk to them." She opened the door wider.

"Look, I don't want to be involved. I just thought Peter needed to know. If he loves her, he might want to help." Cal stepped cautiously through the front door.

Once settled in the parlor, the two detectives questioned him at length about the incident. He told them the same story he told the other detectives at the school.

One rather serious looking investigator asked, "Who is Peter Kirby? Has he got something to do with this kidnapping?"

Cal shook his head firmly. "No, nothing at all. You see Ruth and Peter are in love, but he chose to marry someone else, and Ruth ended up at the boarding school for women. It's odd, but I have this feeling something isn't quite right. Ruth loves him, and if I were a betting man, I would say Peter loves her. Can't quite put my finger on it, but I sure would like to talk to him."

The detective looked at Mrs. Squire. "Why haven't you told us about Peter Kirby, ma'am? Might shed some light on the situation."

"I … well …" She placed both hands over her face and began to weep. "I thought the school could provide the security she needed. Peter tried to find her, but I wouldn't communicate with him. Once again, I was trying to undo the first mistake I made."

Cal gaped at the sobbing woman. "You mean, Peter doesn't know where she is—you didn't tell him?"

Mrs. Squire's shoulders shook as the tears increased. "No, he hasn't any idea."

One of the detectives stood. "I'm confused. An explanation is in order here." He offered a handkerchief. "Start talking, Mrs. Squire."

She dabbed her eyes and explained about the arrangement of marriage. "I wasn't thinking about her happiness at first, only avoiding trouble. Times are so dangerous. My thought was to provide the safeguard of a home and family, a husband to protect her. I was surprised when she actually fell in love with Peter, but the banker destroyed everything. We had to choose to save our home, instead of our daughter's happiness. Eric Horton demanded her hand in marriage and he would balance the second mortgage on our home. It is shameful, I know. When we saw Peter and Ruth in love, well, our decision changed. But, Hattie showed up, and once more, our plans crashed around us."

Cal looked up at the mention of Hattie. "Morgenstern? Is her last name Morgenstern?"

Priscilla hesitated. "Why, yes, I believe that is her name. She lost her family and came to the states to marry Peter. They were betrothed since childhood. Ruth thinks Hattie and Peter will wed, and I allowed the assumption, I'm afraid. How do you know her?"

"Never mind…did you tell Mr. Horton *their* engagement was off, also?"

She nodded.

Cal rose. "I must find Peter and get him to the school. Where is he, Mrs. Squire?"

"Wait just a minute, young man. We are in charge of this investigation. You don't need to take matters into your own hands." The older detective shook a finger at Cal.

"One of you come with me, then. We can find him together. It's important we hurry. Horton could be behind the whole thing. If he was ready to foreclose on the Squires to get their daughter, he's capable of anything."

The detectives looked at one another and gave a quick nod.

◆◆◆◆

Cal hurried out the door with one investigator behind him. "She said he has a milk route in this part of town. Let's start two streets down, it's still early, maybe we'll catch up with him."

They sprinted for the motorcar, and Cal slid into the driver's seat. Ten minutes later, he turned down several streets without spotting the milk truck.

"We could be on the wrong side of his route. He might have already been on these streets." The detective offered.

"We should have split up, but that can't be helped now. I'm gonna try one more street before we drive to the other side." Cal turned the corner. "There he is!"

At the end of the block, a milk truck was parked in front of a large white house, and a man carried milk containers toward the porch. Cal pulled up behind and jumped out of the auto. "Peter? Are you Peter Kirby?"

The empty bottles rattled in the metal container as the man hesitated. "Who are you?"

Cal reached out a hand. "My name is Cal Taylor—from Barkley's School for Women. Ruth is in danger. I think you can help."

"Ruth? You know where she is? I've searched and searched for her. Her parents won't even talk to me." Peter rushed toward Cal.

"She is at the boarding school. Mrs. Squire sent her there. There has been a kidnapping, but they got the wrong girl. They wanted Ruth. We must get to the school. Can you come with us?"

"I have to get the horses back to the house. I can't leave them." Peter looked at both men.

"I understand. Detective can you take my motorcar back to the Squires? Explain the situation, and I will meet you back there. I'll ride with Peter and relay the whole story." Cal handed the keys over.

"Well, I don't know about this. Seems Peter Kirby might be a suspect. Don't think I should let him out of my sight." The investigator scratched his double chin.

"Oh wait," Cal shouted. "Mrs. Whitewood...I almost forgot. I am supposed to pick her up from down the street."

Peter turned around. "You know Mrs. Whitewood—from the Boarding House?"

"Yes, and I know Hattie Morgenstern, too. Met her last night. We were to meet at the bank so she can take Mrs. Whitewood home. Look detective, my mother is the head mistress at the school." He fished a card out of his pocket. "Here is the number. Call her and check me out. I promise I am one of the good guys."

"Well ..."

Cal jumped on the wagon and motioned for Peter. "Let's go, we're wasting time."

Peter hopped up and urged the team into a trot. They left the detective standing in the road, keys dangling in his hand.

"You better start explaining all this to me, Mr. Taylor. Ruth is mine, and I intend to fight for her." Peter flicked the rein a little harder.

"No need to scrap with me, Peter. I know you are the one she loves, but I care enough to want her safe. Let me start at the beginning."

Chapter Twenty-Eight

Priscilla Squire sat in the parlor with the lone detective…silent, tears evaporated. She knew the right thing to do. Robert took the motorcar to the school to be with Ruthie, and knew it was good he was gone. The confession wouldn't set well with him. She lifted her head to speak, but the door flew open.

The second lawman rushed into the room. "We found him. Mr. Taylor is riding with Kirby to take the horses home, and will meet us back here. The man seems honest enough. I don't think he had anything to do with the kidnapping."

"That's not for us to decide, Harry. He is a suspect until we unravel this thing. I personally think the Horton guy did it, but I can't prove it."

Priscilla Squire held up one hand. "You are both wrong, detectives. If you will listen, I can give you the name of the man responsible."

"You know who did it, Mrs. Squire? Why have you let us run in circles when you knew all along?" The tall investigator's voice took a menacing tone.

"Well, I'm not one hundred percent certain, but it is the best possibility at the moment."

"Start talkin' and make it fast." He lit a large cigar stub and leaned against the mantle.

"It's a very long story, detective. To understand, I would have to begin twenty years ago."

The man shook his head. "All I want is a name. Give me the name of the man who did the kidnapping."

"All right, his name is Captain…"

Sarah burst into the room. "Ms. Squire, there are men at the door. Officers—they want to talk with ya, say it's urgent."

The sheriff forced Sarah aside. "No time for pleasantries, ma'am. There's been a shooting. A body surfaced this morning. I need all available men. Harry, that means you and Sam. This takes priority."

"A shooting? Where?" Harry asked.

"Down at the river, near The Blue Feather. Come on, no time to waste." The sheriff bolted for the door, the men scrambled behind.

"Someone was shot? Sarah, did they say who…a man or a girl?" Priscilla raced to the open door and watched them speed away.

"No ma'am, 'fraid I didn't hear which. I surely hope it wasn't that poor child." Sarah said over Priscilla's shoulder.

"I suppose we will hear when they return. We've nothing to do but wait, bring me a cup of tea, Sarah."

"Yes, ma'am."

After the maid left, Priscilla paced the room. *I almost gave them the Captain's name. If Robert knew, he would leave me. I have to think this over.*

◆◆◆◆

Peter gave his mother a quick explanation of the story Cal Taylor recounted. She looked distraught as they hurried out the door, but he would have to worry about that later. Ruth was in danger, and he must find her.

"So, she's been at the school all this time. It never crossed my mind. I figured they hid her so they could arrange the marriage to Eric Horton. He has to be the one behind all this." The steering wheel responded more slowly than he wished as he sped down the country lane and knew impatience was to blame.

"She looked so lost at the train station. I sensed a tragic event brought her to us." Cal kept his eyes straight ahead. "I asked her to a dance, you know. It took some doing, but finally she agreed. That's when I knew her heart would never be mine, it belonged to you."

"Look, the police cars are gone. I wonder what happened." Peter pulled to the curb. Both men jumped out and hurried up the steps.

"Mrs. Squire, Mrs. Squire!" Simultaneously, they pounded on door.

Sarah opened it quickly. "They be gone, Peter. A shooting…at the river, near The Blue Feather."

"Who was shot? Hurry Sarah, tell me." Peter shook her by shoulders.

"They didn't say. Please, I don't know any more."

Cal grabbed Peter's arm. "She doesn't know. Let her go. We know it's not Ruth. We have to keep our wits about us."

Peter removed his hands. "I'm sorry, Sarah. It's just…I'm so close to finding her. Why didn't you come and tell me and save me all this crazy grief?"

Sarah hung her head. "Ms. Squire wouldn't let me. She threatened my job if I told. I'm sorry. I just knew you wouldn't marry that Hattie lady."

Cal's eyes popped. "You mean you considered it?"

"Yes, I mean, no, it's all a mistake." Peter raked his fingers through his hair.

Mrs. Squire stepped into the hallway. "Please gentleman, stop all this badgering. Someone was shot. It could be that poor girl."

Peter whirled around. "You are the cause of all this. If anything happens to *anyone* it is because of your interference."

Cal stepped in between them. "Peter, that won't help—water under the bridge. Let's focus on what we can do to keep Ruth safe and find poor Ella."

"What *can* we do? I need to see Ruth and explain. She needs to know I am in love with her, not Hattie." Peter's hands clenched. "Enough of this, I'm headed to the school."

Cal chased after him. "Wait, I only meant to find you. Go to the school if you must, but I want to find out what happened to Ella. You're on your own, Peter."

Chapter Twenty-Nine

Ruth's fingers stiffened—numb from the cold. The heater in the motorcar didn't work, and the winter air finally seeped into her bones. The long drive from the school depleted her energy, but determination fueled the fire to find Ella. "What are you waiting for, Father? We must find The Blue Feather."

Robert Squire left the gear in park. "Look, Ruthie, the sun is coming up. It won't be long before the café on the edge of town is open. I'm starved. We need to talk about what we are doing. Ella could end up dead if we make a wrong move. I don't want that on my head." With head bowed, he continued. "I think we need to tell the police what we know."

"No, it might be too late."

He shook his head. "I am not budging until you agree. For once, I'm putting my foot down. The police can investigate The Blue Feather. The place is notorious for murders. Every day there is a new one in the newspaper."

"But..."

"No, buts, Ruthie. We're going to the police station and tell them what we know, and then we're going to eat breakfast."

♦♦♦♦

"So, let me get this straight. You accusin' Eric Horton, the banker, of kidnapping some girl at Barkley's?" The police sergeant rolled a pencil across the report and back again, a smile flickered on his lips.

Ruth didn't like the look of the uniformed officer, regardless of the brass buttons and stripes. He was fat and had bad breath. "Look, a young woman's life is in danger. You have to get down to The Blue Feather. Chances are she's already dead."

"What does a girl like you know about The Blue Feather? You don't look the type."

"Fine, if you won't take me seriously, I'll have to go myself." She stood; ready to bolt for the door.

"Hold your horses, lady. You ain't goin' nowhere." He motioned for an officer to stop her. "We'll head down to The Blue Feather, but you won't go near the place. Understand?"

"Inspector, I am her father, and I can attest the story is correct. A young lady was kidnapped from the Barkley School." Robert Squire stepped forward, breaking the promise to let Ruth handle the situation. "Police have been to the school. The worst part is the girl was taken by mistake. They wanted my Ruth."

A messenger handed a note to the sergeant and stood by nervously as he read it. "There's been a shooting, Sarge. Near the river, like she said. Not far from The Blue Feather. It was called into the other precinct."

"I can read. Seems like you're tellin' the truth."

A commotion in the outer office distracted the small group.

"What's goin' on?" the sergeant demanded.

The leader of the intrusion snapped the order. "A kidnapping and a shooting. One dead. We need all available officers."

The scene before her faded and the urge to scream surfaced. She fought for control. "Shooting? Who?"

Mr. Squire stood close, a steady hand on her back. "Can you tell us more, officer? Was it a man or woman?"

"Can't say. Just know we gotta get down there and surround the buildings. It happened less than an hour ago." He spun around and motioned for the rest to follow.

One lone officer remained at the desk, and Ruth realized everyone had forgotten about her. "Let's go, Father. Looks like we are free to leave."

Mr. Squire led her out the front door. "Ruthie, there is nothing we can do now. We would only be in the way. Let's get something to eat, and let the officers do their jobs."

"Father, I..."

"We will hear soon enough. Come along."

◆◆◆◆

Peter watched Cal drive in the direction of the river. *What has that girl to do with me? I need to get to Ruth. He doesn't need me.* The motorcar roared and backed up, ready to head for the country, but the sight of Cal's disappearing coupe ignited a pang of remorse.

Damn! He turned the wheel and followed. *Cal came all this way to warn me. The least I can do is help him find her. Ruth is safe at school with guards round the clock.*

In no time, Peter closed the gap, and the wharf loomed ahead in the morning sunrise. *I am probably going to regret this.*

"Change your mind, Peter?" Cal jumped out of the auto and swung the door shut; a grin danced on his face, but quickly disappeared.

Peter walked around the end of the vehicle and stood beside Cal, eyes on the commotion a block away. "Well—you were kind enough to come all this way, it's the least I can do. Looks like every police officer in the city is down there. What do you make of it?"

"Might be more than one body. I hope Ella isn't one of them. Come on; let's see what we can find out."

They approached the building on the outside edge of the crowded scene. An officer held up his hand. "No one past this point. Nothing to see here. Move along."

"Who was shot? Man or woman?" Cal asked.

"Not at liberty to say. You got no business here, now leave before I arrest *you*." The officer smacked a billy club against his empty hand.

"Sure officer, only curious. We're on our way." Peter pulled Cal toward their autos. "Come on, Cal. We can't do anything now. I need to get to Ruth."

"You go on. I have to stay until I see the body. My mother is the headmistress of the school. Ella is her responsibility, and until I find if she is dead or alive, I'm not budging." He slid onto the hood of the coupe and crossed his arms.

Peter sighed and joined him.

◆◆◆◆

The police had the situation under control, Ruth knew. If they interfered now, Ella could pay the price. Although Father made sense, she gave up the fight, reluctantly. Another idea sprung into head. "Father, do you remember as we drove into town a boarding house called Mrs. Whitewood's?"

"Vaguely, why?"

They walked arm in arm along the sidewalk.

"Peter mentioned Hattie Morgenstern took a room at Mrs. Whitewood's boarding house. It's the same one, I'm sure of it. She convinced him to marry her, and I want to know how. You owe me that much. Please?" Ruth quickened her step.

The hesitation in his step surprised her, and she noticed a pained look cross his face.

"I'm not sure that is a good idea, Ruth. Leave it be. You are in school. We were wrong to manipulate your life. Besides, your mother is home alone right now and probably worried into a frenzy. Let's go home and tell her what is happening. We need to be together as a family now." He stopped next to the motorcar.

"I promise I will drop the matter once I've talked to Hattie. We need to talk woman to woman. I'll return to school and study hard once I resolve this in my mind, you'll see."

He sighed. "Promise?"

She nodded vigorously.

◆◆◆◆

The lump in Ruth's throat grew bigger. *Do I really have the nerve to talk to this woman?* It was too late, however. Father had already knocked on the door.

"It's a might early to be gettin' a room. What do you want?" the white-headed matron snapped.

"Is Miss Morgenstern here? We would like to see her, if it is convenient." Mr. Squire asked.

"Mighta known it was for her. She's had quite a few visitors of late. Hold on." The door shut.

Ruth could hear Hattie's name called and smiled at the impatience in the old woman's voice.

A moment later, Hattie stood before them, surprise in her eyes. "Mr. Squire, Ruth? What are you doing here?"

"May we come in, Miss Morgenstern? I'd like to ask you a question." Ruth found it hard to look at the woman who stole Peter away.

"Certainly, but I'm not sure we have anything to discuss, and Mrs. Whitewood isn't feeling well. I had to bring her home early from our errands."

As Hattie stepped aside, Ruth noticed the dark brown cloak around her shoulders. "Are you going out, again?"

"Oh, not now. I have a luncheon engagement later on. We only arrived home a few moments ago." The cloak landed on a chair inside the parlor as she ushered them inside. "Now, please tell me why you are here."

Ruth sat next to her father at one end of the room. "Miss Morgenstern, I know you are going to marry Peter, and I want to know what you said to turn him away from me. Youth and experience are the most obvious reasons, but he seemed very sincere in his feelings toward me."

Hattie stood and crossed the room, took Ruth's hands in hers, and smiled. "Ruth, Peter has been looking everywhere for you. He is beside himself with frustration. He and I are not going to marry, dear. You ran out before we could finish the announcement." She turned to look at Mr. Squire. "You should be ashamed of yourself. Why didn't you tell her?"

Ruth shook, trying to comprehend the words coming from Hattie's mouth. "Not marry? You and Peter are not going to wed?" For a split second, she continued the gaze into the woman's eyes. Slowly, her attention focused on her father. "Father … you knew about this? You sent me to Barkley's knowing Peter wasn't going to marry Miss Morgenstern? How could you?"

Before Mr. Squire could react, Hattie intervened. "Barkley's school? You've been at Barkley's all this time? Then you know about the kidnapping."

"How did you know about that? It only happened last night! It couldn't have been in the newspapers, yet." Ruth stood and released Hattie's grasp.

"A young man took a room here last night. He said he had come from the school to find a man who could help protect the young lady the crooks were really after. Oh my gosh, is it you, Ruth?"

"What was the man's name?"

"Cal—Cal Taylor."

All three stood in the middle of the room, silent, mouths half open, eyes wide.

Finally, Ruth spoke. "Cal came looking for Peter? Is that what you are saying?"

"He never mentioned his name, but from what I can see now, that is correct. You know Cal?"

"Yes, his mother runs the school. Hattie, this is awful. If Cal came to find him, then Peter must know about the kidnapping. Cal will try to find Ella, I know it, and Peter, being the kind of man he is, will try to help him." She whirled on her father. "You just may have gotten Peter and Cal killed! We have to get down to The Blue Feather."

Chapter Thirty

Cal Taylor watched the activity at the wharf intently. Even though he wasn't allowed closer, he saw the stretcher when the draped body was brought out. A crowd of policemen and detectives obscured the view. His heart drummed harder, and breathing stopped.

He couldn't stand it, he had to know. Impulse took over; he slid off the motorcar and ran toward the crowd.

A shout stopped him in his tracks. "She's alive!" A minute later, the curly blonde head of Ella Adams bobbed up and down in the crush of people. His heart soared.

Peter jumped off the auto. "Can you see her? My God, that is wonderful. But who was shot?" He paused. "Cal, we have to find out who died. The kidnapper might still be out there."

"You're right, let's try to get closer. We can sneak around the side of that building."

Peter grabbed his arm. "Look…over there."

About a block away, two women hurried toward them, waving, their voices ever louder as they approached.

"Cal, it's Ruth, and Hattie is with her." Peter broke into a run and scooped Ruth into his arms. "Is it really you? I thought I lost you forever."

"Peter," she breathed. "I thought you were going to marry Hattie. I couldn't stay and watch. My parents sent me to boarding school, and…"

"Never mind that now. Ella was found alive, but the kidnapper might still be out there. We know he wanted *you*. It's not safe here. We need to leave." Peter guided her away from the wharf.

"Wait, look Peter. There's a big commotion by the river's edge." Cal ran toward the abandoned building. No one paid attention as he inched around the building and wiggled his way into the crush of reporters and lawmen.

"It's another body—looks like a man. We've got another murder on our hands." A gruff voice announced.

Cal pressed closer. "Anyone know who it is?" He whispered into the crowd.

A loud shout pierced the air. "Hey, it's that banker, Eric Horton. Looks like he was shot in the head."

Cal pressed harder into the crowd. "I wonder if he's the kidnapper. But who killed *him*?"

The reporter next to him answered, "That's the question, isn't it sonny? We may never know."

"Hey, do you know the other victim?" Cal took advantage of the reporter's loose tongue.

"They say it's Audie Zuckerman. Big mob boss in these parts."

Peter shouted at Cal. "The women aren't safe here, Cal. Let's go."

Cal smiled and waved back. "I'm coming." It did him good to see Ruth and Peter, arms linked, not a speck of daylight between them. *I just knew those two belonged together.*

A glint of light flickered in the upper story window of the run down building on the corner. He caught a glimpse of a man ducking past the open aperture and felt a pang of alarm. *I must be jumpy. Nothing there.*

"Did you find out anything?" Peter pulled Ruth forward to catch up to Cal.

"Uh, yeah. They said the man in the river was some banker. Horton, I think. The guy in the alley was a big mob boss, named Audie Zuckerman." Cal looked over his shoulder at the empty window. "You're right, let's get out of here, this no place for the ladies."

Ruth gasped and sank to her knees. "Eric Horton! Oh, my God … Audie was his driver. How could he be a mob boss?"

Peter grabbed Cal's arm. "Did you say Horton? Eric Horton?"

"Didn't hear a first name. Look Peter, I saw someone in the window up there. Looked like he could have a gun. Let's go. We need to get Ruth and Hattie out of here."

Both men pulled Ruth to her feet.

"Father is in the motorcar down the block. We need to make sure he's okay." Ruth's voice was almost inaudible.

"Let's go back to Ruth's house. The killer might head that way." Cal turned to Hattie. "Peter will take care of Ruth, Hattie would you mind riding with me?"

Hattie nodded and took his arm.

◆◆◆◆

"What is going on down there, Ruthie? I heard the shouting. Peter it's good to see you." Robert Squire sat behind the wheel of his auto.

"Mr. Squire, we need to get back to your house immediately. Two men were killed; one of them is Eric Horton."

Ruth's father blanched white. "Peter, my wife is alone at the house. Hurry!"

◆◆◆◆

Priscilla Squire sat in the darkened parlor drapes drawn, hands folded. *What have I done? First Ruthie, and now poor Ella. I pray she is alive. Why oh why, didn't I leave things alone? My life was good, and I was blind to it.*

A knock on the door revived her from the abstraction. She waited for Sarah to answer it, but the knock continued, louder, and more forceful. *Maybe it's news about Ella. I should answer it.*

The door swung open, and Priscilla Squire fought to stay on her feet. In the doorway, stood an old adversary, disheveled, a wild gleam in his eye and a gun pointed at her heart. "Hello Priscilla. It's been too long since we last met. I believe we have some unfinished business."

The scream died in her throat as she whispered, "Alexander."

The End

Made in the USA
Columbia, SC
01 July 2022